THERE WE HAVE BEEN

Leland Bardwell

44 East Essex Street, Dublin 2, Ireland.

© Leland Bardwell

First published in Ireland in 1989 by
Attic Press Ltd.
44 East Essex Street
Dublin 2

British Library Cataloguing in Publication Data
Bardwell, Leland
    There we have been.
    I. Title
    838'.914 [F]

    ISBN 0-946211-81-7

Cover Design: Paula Nolan
Cover Illustration: Geraldine O'Reilly
Printing: Camelot Press
Typesetting: Phototype-Set Ltd., Dublin

The publishers acknowledge the assistance of The Arts Council/An Chomhairle Ealaíon who grant aided this book. The author was assisted by the "Authors Royalty Scheme Loan" of The Arts Council/An Chomhairle Ealaíon.

'I can only say, there we have been: but I cannot say where and I cannot say how long, for that is to place it in time.'

T.S. Eliot

LELAND BARDWELL was born in India of Irish parents. Her novels include *Girl on a Bicycle, That London Winter* and *The House.* Her first collection of short stories, *Different Kinds of Love,* was published by Attic Press in 1987

For my three sons, Nicholas, Edward and John.

ACKNOWLEDGEMENTS

I wish to thank Mary and Bernard Loughlin for their friendship and hospitality throughout my stay in and around the Tyrone Guthrie Centre, and especially for the time spent in Maggie's Cottage wherein this book was largely written. I also wish to thank my co-cottager Geraldine (author O.R. Melling) for her loyalty and good humour during that time.

PROLOGUE

CONSTANCE

This account of the meetings between Cathy and Constance took place in a middle-sized town somewhere in Northern Ireland sometime in the eighties.

'These are your brother's hands, and your father's, the hands that blinded me . . .'

Sophocles

Doctor Le Strange wished the telephone would stop ringing.

For the last few years she had been living on brandy more or less.

Any time away from her scribbling pad or her bottle she considered wasted.

She glanced at her most recent entry: 'I'm supposed to believe in normality but I can only love the casualties, the unbeautiful.' She bent down and opened a drawer while picking up the receiver with the other hand.

'I'm not in,' she yelled, jamming the phone back on its cradle.

She continued to write, the new bottle of brandy unwrapped and ready for pouring.

'Imagination, ie transference of acute observation to the psyche, ends with childhood. What we call imagination thereafter is an intellectual culling up of images. Poets make a career out of this, upholstering lines to fit the medium. My patients inhabit their own metaphors. My muses, Thalia and Melpomene, I trust in, to steer me through these labyrinthine years. Passages between madness ecstatic and madness repelling, meso-madness and madness metaleptic (more often called schizophrenia).'

The telephone rang again.

Furious, she picked it up.

'What now?'

'Look, Constance, I've someone for you. Someone who can really help you.'

'I'm perfectly fine the way I am.'

'No you're not. And you know it,' the voice continued.

'Well, what's your latest scheme to get me back?'

'A girl. Well not a girl, really. She's a young twenty-two. She has been looking for someone. I think you'll be interested.'

'Christ, Jim.'

'John.'

'John, I don't want any member of the deprived cluttering up my room. I'm busy.' She put the receiver down.

She wrote: 'Gradgrind.'

Now who was he, she wondered. Out of what well of darkness had she dragged this name?

She took a swig from the bottle, forgetting to pour it out in her excitement. A book. A big red book. Dickens. Selfishness. *Hard Times.*

How appropriate, she thought. To what?

She had an idea.

She picked up the phone and dialled the Centre.

'Can I speak to Jim, the chief psychiatrist?'

'There is no Jim here, madam. Would it be Dr John McKay?'

'Yes, yes. Of course.'

She waited while the woman went to fetch him. When his hello crackled over the line, she said, 'Fuck you.'

'That's Constance, isn't it?'

'Of course it is.'

'What's the matter? Are you drunk?'

'No, of course I'm not drunk. That's the trouble. Well. This girl, woman, delinquent. You want to pick my brains. But you know I have no brains.' When the voice made a clucking sound, she said,

'Yes, you fucking well know what's wrong with me.'

'It's only delayed shock. You'll get over it.'

'And if I don't want to?'

'It's up to you.' John McKay was a patient man but his temper was short. 'I'll send her round to you.'

However, at the moment he was excited. Quite by chance this young woman had been sent to him. Her story was extraordinary. Apparently she was searching for a friend. A woman of about Constance's age. And it might, just might, if Constance used her old techniques, cause an enormous change in her condition. It might be the counter-shock she needed.

'I see,' said Constance, 'the lamb to the slaughter.'

'Exactly. Four o'clock tomorrow then. And Constance?'

'What?'

'Please let her in.' He rang off.

Two days later Cathy Magee arrived.

'What's the name of your lipstick?' Le Strange asked.

'Dunno.'

'If it has a name. It doesn't suit you.'

'Sorry.' Cathy was still standing in the doorway.

'Sit down.' The girl obeyed.

Doctor Le Strange took no more notice of her. She began leafing through old entries in her note-book. She read:

'Under my sequestering aegis, they scavenge for my sympathy. I cannot refute what they say because of my salary which keeps me in the luxury to which I am accustomed. They arrive, unasked, reeking of paranoia, nerves under siege.'

'Yes, now,' she addressed Cathy. 'What seems to be the matter?'

'It's Dilly, miss. I'm looking for Dilly. I must find her.'

'I see. And what have you done to find her?'

'I heard she was hiding out in a hotel, in Dublin. I went there.'

'I see.'

There was another long silence. Constance scribbled.

'They send me this Cathy. They sick her up on me.' She looked over at her. 'She chain-smokes.'

The doctor got up and went to the window. A small black car was parked up the street on a double yellow line. She went back to her desk and wrote: 'This unfortunate child who is not a child finds me at the watershed of my life. My body is no longer free. Extremes of heat and cold affect me. I sleep sporadically and have mournful dreams.'

She began to sing:

'Walking back to happiness with you...ou...'

'I know that song, miss. A man sang it when I was in hospital. Dilly said it was a very old song. She knew it as a child.'

'And this Dilly? What is she?'

'Reynold's sister, miss. She gave me money, a little, to get a job.'

'And did you get a job?'

'No. I couldn't. I tried. I did really.'

'Do you know,' the doctor said, 'that I have only a pension to live on? I am not a practising doctor any more. When I...when it ... the National Health Service doled me out a pension. Enough to keep me in brandy and biros. Did you know that, Cathy?' The other squirmed uncomfortably, not knowing what to say. 'Say something, Cathy. Do you know why you're here?'

'They told me you'd cure me.'

'That's a good one.'

Cathy went silent again.

'Did they not tell you? You're here to cure me. They are crooks, of course.'

'But you're the doctor.'

'Did I not explain? I did, I think.'

'God, miss, what will I do?'

'I've no idea, Cathy. Come back tomorrow.'

Dr Le Strange was looking in the mirror when Cathy came next day. She was looking for something, a likeness or something. Cathy reminded her of someone. Who? Was it herself when young? But no. Her features were all wrong. Cathy's face was dull, expressionless.

'I must have been beautiful, when young,' she wrote.

'Now, Cathy . . . this woman . . .'

'Dilly.'

'Was she good-looking?'

'No, miss ... well, yes ... she was beautiful.'

'Jolie-laide?'

'What?'

'Pretty-ugly.'

Cathy began to hate Constance: she wanted to go back to the Centre. There was something going on here that she couldn't understand. But Constance was laughing now, striding back and forth across the room.

'Go on, Cathy, tell me. Was she old?'

'Yes.'

'As old as I am?'

'Dunno.'

'Fifty, sixty?'

'Oh, God, miss, not that old.'

Constance sat down abruptly. Her head was reeling. She snatched the bottle and drank from the neck. She looked at Cathy. Within her vision the young woman began to change ... to change subtly. She saw her as she would be in thirty years. There was something. What was it? Then she jerked herself up. What had happened? She'd caught a glimpse of something. All these somethings ... tiny snapshots. That crook McKay was trying to trap her into a cure.

'But of course,' she heard her voice rise. 'There is no cure.'

That was a comforting thought. But Cathy interrupted.

'Please, miss. They told me at the Centre that you'd ... '

'Yes?'

'Oh, I don't know. Understand. I want to get Dilly back to the farm.'

'Farm? First I've heard of a farm.'

There was a long silence.

Constance began to study her again. She looked at her lipstick (purple today. Less obnoxious, Constance thought). She looked at her bright blue acrylic jumper, her tight black silky pants, her high-heeled plastic boots. She looked at her large face. She found nothing there any more. That momentary glimpse had almost revealed an ... image ... almost. An image, a snapshot ... 'Farm,' she muttered to herself.

'Please, can I go?'

Constance dragged herself out of her reverie. 'What? Oh ... wait.'

Cathy looked longingly towards the door but didn't dare get up.

'Your father beat you?'

'How do you know?'

Cathy sat up, fear darkening her cheeks.

'Perhaps I am a wizard. That sort of thing is on the cards.'

'Well,' she continued when the other said nothing. 'What do you want?'

'I've told you. Dilly.'

'So you think I'm a magician. Can produce this ... Dilly ... at the drop of a hat.'

'Oh no, miss.'

'Well, what have you done to find her yourself?'

'I went looking for her in that hotel.'

'Well?'

'When I pressed the bell a dwarf came out. Put the fear of God in me. He was no bigger than me chest.'

Constance yawned. 'What colour was the bell?'

'Blue.'

'Ah. Blue bell.' She paused, stretched out her beautifully-manicured nails. 'You went in? With the dwarf?'

'I followed him in. He rolled up the steps in front of me.'

'Rolled? Like a sailor.'

Constance began to scribble: 'Short legs and long body. Genghis Khan. All those hordes.'

'He cut through Europe like a knife,' she said aloud.

'I beg your pardon?'

'Genghis Khan. Where they went — the hordes — they impregnated the local women. So their offspring all had short legs and long bodies.' Constance was laughing at her own madness now. Laughing uncontrolledly. Only by taking a massive swig from the bottle was she able to calm her outburst.

'I don't understand.' Cathy was trying not to cry. This woman didn't give a damn. She wanted to leave so much but all her energy had left her.

'Carry on. Was she there?'

'Oh, miss. The place was awful. I booked in for the night. I couldn't find my room for ages. There was no Dilligence Strong in the register. Only a Mr and Mrs Starling that might be her. The place smelled something awful. When I did find my room it was so small I could hardly shut the door. And no lock on it.'

'It was a dump.' Constance suddenly came to her senses. 'A fucking dump.'

'I left my room and went down to the sittingroom. To see if she was there. But there was a lot of girls with fat arms and furry jumpers and soft breasts. And two old ones. Man and wife. He held the telly control in his hand and kept flicking from station to station. They all had their eyes glued to the box.'

Constance noticed that the young woman had begun to shake. Perhaps she should send her back. Tell that crook McKay that the whole business was a canard. The girl was round the twist anyway.

The one word, Farm, kept haunting her. She wrote: 'Farm. A farm is a place where terrible feuds are enacted. Where brothers kill brothers for a forkful of hay. So naturally any dump would be preferable.' She smiled.

'I take it,' she said carefully, 'this woman ... Dilly ... wasn't there.'

'Please listen, miss. It was so awful afterwards. While I was standing in the doorway I was pushed. Honest to God. I went sprawling on to the carpet. I could smell the dust and see the old one's slippers near my nose and her coarse ankles. I struggled up but it was worse standing because a huge man was right in front of me laughing. He had wide shoulders and long arms like a gorilla. But his hands were dainty. He had manicured fingers. He bent over me, his lip drawn into a toothless mouth. Laughing. Great saddles of laughter coming out of his chest.' Cathy's face began to stipple as if withholding laughter herself now. 'He said he wanted to read my stars and the old couple were both Libra and pointing to the girls he reeled off their different birth signs and he said he guessed I was Aries because I was light and skinny. He brought out an old paper and read out my stars for the week. It was all complicated. Like a pattern of happenings. I felt he was putting strings into my head, I was that confused and frightened. I'd backed into an armchair and his shins were against mine and he was leering down at me. Somehow I knew . . . I don't know how . . . that he must have something to do with Dilly. And then . . . Oh miss . . . She came in. I didn't recognise her at first, she looked so awful . . . like a witch . . . hair all askew, a crazy look in her eyes . . . she tried to drag him out but he swivelled on her and produced a bottle of soapy water and started to force her to drink it. She kept screaming at him but he held the bottle in her mouth . . . like drenching a calf . . . the liquid bubbled all down her chin. Eventually he emptied the rest on the floor and marched her out. I kept screaming "Dilly" but she just looked through me. And none of them took a blind bit of notice. Just kept on watching the box like they had the needle. They must have booked in as Mr and Mrs Starling . . . '

Cathy looked over at the doctor. She tried to see if she had understood anything. But Constance's head was lowered over her notebook and she was scribbling furiously. When at last she looked up, she said: 'So I take it that was that. You left like anyone in your shoes would have done.'

'Oh no, miss. No. I had to get her alone. I was determined. My old Dilly was somewhere there. I'd get her to go back. To leave this man. But oh God, the rest is worse.'

'Priapic?'

'What?'

'Priapus, the god of procreation.' Constance yawned. A terrible lethargy was bearing down on her. She wanted Cathy to leave. This story was a shambles. About some old woman selling out to a psychopath. It had nothing to do with her. Or had it? The story's as old as the hills. Then she suddenly saw Cathy as if for the first time, huddled, timid but somewhere under that surface of humility lurked a profound need for love ...

She, like many another, would sacrifice everything to achieve these dizzy heights ... but how misdirected ... Is not all such emotional craziness misdirected? Look at her there. A coloured plastic doll without a ghost of a chance. Although she felt almost gentle towards her, just then she wanted more than anything to be alone.

'Go now, Cathy.' She could detect a beseeching note in her own speech now. 'Perhaps in a few weeks' time we can have another chat.'

Cathy rose, limp, defeated. She would go back to the Centre and rot, she supposed. She wished she had never come, never met this Constance whoever-she-was. She shuffled to the door and Constance listened carefully to her receding steps.

She got up and went to the window. Old women spend much time looking out of windows, she told herself. She watched Cathy going up the street, which was quite empty at this hour. The houses across the road had that dignified look like a row of maiden aunts — would do their best never to interfere in other people's lives. It was strange to think that when night came people scurried around within those walls. Like moles perhaps who dread the light of day.

She went back to her seat and pouring herself a measure of brandy with her left hand she began to scribble: 'Starlings. They obscure the sun like a cloud when they are on the wing.' She took a swig and finished off with 'c.f. Whooper swans'.

DILLY'S STORY

On the 25th June 1979 Mr Jim Strong
died. He left his property to his
children, Reynold, Constance and
Dilligence. The property consisted
of 75 acres of land and a two-storied
dwelling house situated near Mullaghbawn
some six miles south of the Border.

'Lonely lonely, lonely, lonely,
A story with a middle only ... '
                    Paul Durcan

'I don't know what happened to
my face but it don't hurt none.'
                    Dizzy Gillespie

I was so keyed up to see my old home that I hardly listened to
the complaints of the taxi driver. He moaned continuously about
the condition of the roads as if I'd dug the holes in them myself.
Complained also about the built-in obsolescence of foreign
motor cars — all recycled stuff — and lectured me on the
necessity to travel light. (Without a bicycle is what he meant).

When I told him to turn left about a mile and a half outside the
village he didn't believe me. He asked me how long it was since I
was here and when I said, about thirty years, he turned right
round belligerently, as if to say I'm not going up that bloody
boreen.

However, as I said, I didn't care. I paid him his rip-off price and unloaded my gear. At last I was here.

I stood.

I thought, What if *he's* here before me?

It was late July, windy. The clouds shifted and the sun came out and showed up everything that was rotten.

Some windows in the house were broken. (A large bite out of the window of the room in which I used to sleep.) The yard was practically without an angle or a straight line. A gap in the main wall looked as though it had been caused by a river bursting through and drying up quickly afterwards. Boulders were scattered everywhere.

I stood and thought. I thought about my brother, Reynold. I thought about my dead sister, Constance. But I thought mostly about the place.

It was mine! After all these years.

Half mine, anyway.

This was actually the back of the house. I hadn't yet seen the front. Long long ago we had given up using the front of the house. It faced north. Gradually grass grew through the 'front door' and we ignored it. The wood had gone soft. The main sittingroom to the left of the entrance grew cold and damp. Fungi lurked in the corners. We gave up using it and re-established ourselves at the back. An old lumber room beside the kitchen became the new drawingroom and guests were deposited in there instead.

I stood.

Surrounded by my suitcases and bike like someone waiting for a train that has already passed through the station.

Surely he doesn't want this place, I thought. Surely my citified brother would never take on this ramshackle building, this run-down farm. I left my gear and went through the kitchen door.

'What the bloody hell are you doing here?'

Six years since I'd seen him. Long years. Did I expect a change in him? If I did I was foolish.

Reynold has a well-kept body of moderate size, a round head and undistinguished eyes — pale blue. His expression is neither suave nor over-confident, yet he has that disapproving look on him. The kind of look people have when they smell something unpleasant. He has that sort of mauve look to the cheeks, the kind of skin that has seen a lot of shaving, a lot of wear and tear. His tightly-cropped hair covers his head like a brillo-pad. But he favours an untidy moustache.

He is a widower now, with two grown-up daughters (one in

Canada, one in Dublin). Once he was happily married to a small Canadian wife who, I understand, was a perfect housewife and mother. I heard he was sad when she died. Why wouldn't he be, after all?

'The solicitor, Mr Forbes, wrote and told me.'

'Preposterous.'

'Why?'

'You know very well. You should have written. Warned me.'

'If I had written I might have ended up not coming.'

The small battered Rayburn stood, as it had always stood, in the recess of the kitchen. I opened the door and began to riddle it.

'Stop!'

'The prodigal daughter is home. I must clean the flues.'

'For God's sake leave that thing alone. I've spent hours.'

'The whole point. You address it with firm subtlety.'

He poked at his moustache with a blunt forefinger.

'You can't stay. It's out of the question.'

'I can't leave. The last bus has gone.'

'It's no laughing matter. I was just getting used to ... thinking things over ... working things out ... Your shop? What about it? Your London acquaintances? Your alliances? You're over the top ...'

'Reynold. I'm your sister. Constance's sister. Do you remember?'

'Only too well. And don't drag Constance's name into it.'

'I'm not dragging.'

'How long do you plan to stay?'

'How long have any of us at our age? You are older than I, yes, Reynold. How long do you think? Guess.'

'I can't countenance it.'

Countenance: v.t. Favour, support, abet, sanction, approve of, encourage ... No, dear brother, you can't do any of these things.

The kitchen, dark on entering, had become bright once my eyes got used to it. He had sat himself in one of the upright chairs and his body was stiff with dread. This redoubtable city gent was wearing what he imagined was country attire. A mustard-coloured thick cotton shirt under a thin wool pullover (the kind you get in every popular store). His trousers (grey corduroy) were choked into Wellington boots which came right up to his knees.

He looked somewhat like a television caricature of an Anglo-Irish buffer. And yet he wasn't that, at all. All his life he had sat behind a desk administering something. Very middle-class, with never a hint of the old 'landed' stock about him. Back and forth to work in an unflamboyant motor-car. Everything about him was 'middle'. Middle-class, middlebrow, middle of the road politically, middle-aged.

'I'll go to my room,' I said.

The jagged diamond broken from my window had been caused by a bird. Its corpse lay stiffly in its bed of splinters. Its legs shone like paraffin oil, the claws curled as though it had died on a perch. One wing was lifted as a last attempt to fly. It was a young blackbird, orange beak stained, open, the tongue protruding. It had choked to death from thirst.

Because the window sash was broken I had to hold the window up with my shoulder as I leant out, dangling its stiff little body over the sill. I hurled it as far as I could beyond the panorama of missing slates and rusty galvanised roofs, pock-marked outhouses. Some way into the field I could still see the remnants of the haggard, a skeleton of girders and joists as though it had been tossed around by an angry giant. And everything, everything was that little bit smaller than I had expected.

What a mess everything was. Piles of furniture had been thrown into my room — chairs that needed upholstering, legless tables, a chest, missing a drawer. My bed was a mass of old dishes and plates stained from overheating, cups without handles, chipped vases and rusty cutlery. I sat down on the only unbroken chair and tried to laugh.

An hour later, the bed cleared, the mattress shaken out, I descended the stairs to find Reynold in the 'new' sittingroom, kneeling before the grate. The room was neat as though waiting for guests. He was trying to encourage a flame by holding a newspaper in front of the fire. He cursed when the paper flared up and flew up the chimney in lacy black pieces. The fire subsided into a dull glow, wet sticks sending out driblets of sap. Ash shifted.

'It's not that cold, is it?'

'Father lived mainly in here and in his bedroom. I have to keep the place aired.'

'He won't need to be kept warm where he's gone.'

'Dilly.' Reynold swirled around, still on his hunkers.

'Sorry.'

'I'll mortgage the farm and give you your share in cash. You can expand your shop, then.'

'I've sold the lease.'

'Oh my God.'

'We have half shares here, you know.'

'Not you and me. You and me and Constance.'

'Constance is dead.'

'Not to me. Their bodies were never found.'

I discreetly turned to leave the room.

'Wait.'

He was holding a second sheet of newspaper against the embers.

'Why don't we get in the chimney sweep?' I asked.

He bunched up the newspaper and banged it into the coal box.

'Father made his will years ago. He couldn't have known then that Constance would ... disappear.'

'He could have changed it later. He wasn't senile, I gather.'

'He always hoped.'

The daughter made in his image — Constance.

'It's possible father knew in his heart of hearts, but decided to die hoping. On the other hand it would appeal to his sense of humour, knowing how you hated me ...'

'I don't hate you, Dilly. I feel sorry for you.'

'Why?'

'You were always wilful. You are your own worst enemy.'

'My life has been no better nor no worse than anyone else's. Perhaps we can make a bargain. Make a friendly alliance. It has been known. It needs two people to get this place on its feet.'

But all Reynold said was, 'I do think old Forbes should have done something about it when father was making his will.'

'Forbes!'

I had to laugh. I pictured him as a lean young man more than thirty years ago. Even then— on the other hand — he didn't seem young. Eyes like triangles that dipped in the middle into a watery blur. How he must have fussed over father's will. He would never have countermanded an old man's decision.

I wandered out. It was dusk. There had been a shower. The earth smelled like almonds and raisins baking in a cake. I wondered then should I take a U-turn and go back. What had I left in London? My what? My lover? Ex-lover? Lovers?

'Oh keep the dog far hence that's friend to man
        Or with his nails he'll dig it up again.'

Should I write and say, 'There's nothing here for me'?

I looked at the setting sun. Orange, it lit the surroundings, the calcified bark on the orchard trees, the rusty iron gates and tumbledown walls, and I thought about the long years I had waited to return here, always afraid father would sell out before he died. All I had ever dreamed of on the London pavements of time — the emigrant's return! The brown fibre suitcase tied with string, long since crumbled into dust, but these few acres were *mine*.

Half mine, anyway.

I unlatched a rickety gate into a field and it fell on its side.

But Constance didn't die at her own speed.

So father believed — for how many of his last years? Three? — that she had somehow escaped. But if so where was she? Yes, must I now feel sorry for him? True, her knick-knacks, her photographs, the cups she won at school, are all there in the glass case.

No photos of you and me, dear brother, are there?

The hill field, abandoned to the energy of blackthorn and nettles, stretches way up to the further townland of Corragh-bawn and Tullagh — local people could never agree which townland was the biggest so they were amalgamated to save a row. The line at the top of the field is marked by a row of greasy chestnuts, despondent, keeping alive as though by some hidden will.

To the left, what has always been called the 'well' field runs down to the river beyond which a square field of unexampled poverty denotes the end of our land. As little girls, Constance and I had welded fact with fantasy round that well, but long before I left it had dried up, leaving only traces of algae.

I heard Reynold's voice. I knew the call. A sharp breathing-in before letting out an unfriendly bellow. When I got back he was standing in the doorway in a curve, one shoulder holding the hasp, a hand resting on the lintel. I had an urge to link him back into the kitchen but the idea to him would have been 'preposterous'.

'No, Dilly!'

'Please, I'm tired. Can't we leave it till tomorrow?'

'No.'

He piled small squares of rubbery meat and carrots and onions on to two plates.

'You have to eat, I suppose.'

'Yes, I suppose so.'

I unplugged a chunk of meat from a molar. 'Why did you come back?' I asked. 'You had a good job, good income. As far as I remember you hated this place.'

'Property escalates.'

'This land is rack and ruin. You'll need a fortune to get it on its feet.'

'You suddenly sound practical. What about you? Starve here on your own? Is that what you want?'

'I need very little. Peace and time. Things like that.'

'Live like a hermit on peace and time. Pah.'

He ate up everything. All the rubbery meat went down while mine was ringed round the edge of my plate. With a sweep he cleaned up the gravy with a piece of bread and threw the plate into the sink.

'If you want to make tea or coffee the kettle's boiling. Nescafé, I'm afraid. I expect you're too sophisticated for that sort of thing.'

He left the room.

I saw myself then as he sees me. I use his words about myself. I am unpredictable, sly, ugly. I have (or had) unsuitable friends somewhere 'over there'. I dress wrongly. I don't wear coats and flowered dresses. I will disgrace him in the village.

But no, dear brother, I will do nothing of the kind. All that is behind me. Sex and booze and madness. Finished. And friends? What are they? Take a link from a chain and the chain rejoins itself. No. I want nothing. No one. The land is all I want.

He came back in.

'Turn out the light when you go up.'

He took a ledger from the top of the dresser, looked over it at me, eyes bloodshot round the rims.

'Are you not going to bed?'

He left again with the ledger under his arm.

Father didn't inherit this farm. The house is — well — certainly not a mansion. What used to be called a 'strong' farmhouse. He caused the kitchen to be built on at the back and put in the 'modern' cooking range. No. He bought the place on mother's whim. She it was who fancied being squire's wife, had delusions of grandeur, had cards printed with their name and address, 'called' on the local 'gentry'. The address had been a poser at first because the house had no name. It was known locally as McCartan's farm. But this wasn't good enough for mother, so she decided to call it Corraghbawn House. No matter how she tried, however, she never quite made it with 'the quality'. In the thirties and forties there was still a rigid pecking order — even the doctor and solicitor were only invited to tea if they were good at tennis. This snubbing affected her nerves, stirred up an anger in her which thereafter she could never subdue for long. All father wanted was a bit of golf, the odd race-meeting, and golf clubs and racecourses were scarce in this neck of the woods.

When we were born — my sister first and then me (Reynold was already away at boarding school) — we had a modicum of happiness. We were inseparable. We had a secret language. We prefixed each syllable with the three letters ERM and spoke so fast no one else could understand us. Constance, adored and adoring. As a baby, as four, six, seven, eight-year-old — pretty, alluring, silken-haired Constance. Me? I was rough-haired, broad-faced, surly, hating and hated, except by Constance. I kept her affection by working at it night and day. I'd tell her stories to make her sleep, steal sweets for her in the village shop, copy her mannerisms until ... until, I suppose, she grew out of me.

Finally I learnt to roam alone. Soon I forgot. Other things began to take my interest.

She was much in my mind as I sat on into the night. In spite of my exhaustion I had to stay in the kitchen, allowing these memories to circle round my brain. As if there had been no interim period between my leaving and my returning.

Guiltily I heard his footsteps descending the stairs. How quickly he had acquired his moral superiority over me!

'I thought you were tired.'

'I was just thinking.'

'That's what I was afraid of.'

'Father, you know, in spite of his penchant for an easy life, really lorded it around. Aided and abetted by ma, of course. When it came to local working people, they weren't human. They were either "that man" or "that wretched woman".'

'If you persist in these criticisms why do you want to live here?'

'I love this place. I love every blade of grass, every stump of a tree, every joist and girder on the old barn ...'

'Dilly, that's enough. Another thing.'

'What now?'

'Do you always dress like that?' I smiled. 'What are you smiling at?' I shrugged.

'What's wrong with jeans?'

'People like us... at our age ...'

'Who are the people like us? The Hamiltons, the Bissets?'

'The Bisset sisters are dead. The Hamilton house was pulled down and the place is a Co-op now. You see, Dilly, it's different.'

'If it's different, why shouldn't I be different? Really!'

'And you were supposed to be the intelligent one.'

I woke that first morning after a night on the damp lumpy mattress, etiolated but refreshed. When I washed my face from the cold tap in the bathroom (also on the abandoned north side) I noticed the porcelain flowers had already fallen from the rhododendron bushes and lay at their feet as though stitched into the grass. A bird settled amongst the leaves.

'No flowers full of insects, bird, left for you,' I said as the icy water coursed into the neck of the T-shirt in which I had slept.

But first things first, I decided. That meant writing a list of all the local names I remembered, with queries as to whether they still existed.

Mrs Partridge: Protestant. Owner, runner and tyrant in the Licensed Grocers and Vintners trade. In other words boss of the only grocer's shop. Four fat daughters. Three thin sons.

McDonaghs: Neighbouring farmers. Catholic. One large son. Four daughters. All suspicious of us 'Prods'.

Spence, John: Protestant. Son of better off and retired farmers just over the border. Six miles from Ballyvaughan (that's the village, by the way, in case I haven't mentioned it already). Parents very stiff holy Joes from whom I kept as far as possible.

Arthur Begley: Catholic. Different kettle of fish. Very nice. Same age as I. (Great fun).

Bissets: Protestants. Ancient sisters, frail, bepurpled.

Hamiltons: Ditto. More robust. Keen on gardening. Nails always black. Decent with scones and cake. (As heretofore mentioned, all gone or dead).

Rev. McGivern: Detestable clergyman. Sermons often an hour long.

Father J. Daly: Less detestable parish priest.

As I listed these people I was stunned by how I marked the religion of each. How conscious we always were of sectarian differences when things were quiet and the border really a smuggling joke.

It made me uneasy, although my decision to return had not been in the least bit coloured by nervous anticipation. Once back, however, the Protestant/Catholic psyches became a focal point of my brooding.

I re-read the short list and decided to stop there. No doubt other names would gradually swim back into my consciousness.

I breakfasted early and wandered out into the fields. I tried to order my thoughts, to keep to the job in hand. I knew the future was only marginally savable as were the four damp fields. If Reynold and I couldn't pull together we'd starve. (Or kill each other).

At the front of the house dry grass grew right up to the window sills. The ancient monkey-puzzle was still there, obscuring light from our one-time sittingroom. If that side of the house were to be refurbished the tree would have to go. It was hideous anyway, waxy and dusty as an old rubber plant.

Reynold claimed at breakfast that he feared I'd be found dead drunk in the village. I said I had no intention of putting my nose inside the village pub unless accompanied by a friend. (At the word 'friend' he snorted).

'I trust you're not bringing that unsuitable man with whom you associated over here, are you?'

'Man or men?'

'Dilly, you're insufferable. That bird. That married man?'

'I left him.'

The eggs were stale. I suggested hens. Brought on another tirade.

'Typical greenpeace gobbledy-gook! Have you any idea what the feed costs?'

He went off muttering about a chain-harrow salesman.

I wandered down to the river. I caught a glimpse of a girl. A waif-like creature who darted into the woods when she heard me coming. I guessed she'd be about fourteen — although undergrown. I felt all washed up and woebegone myself and sat a while dangling my feet in the water.

This river, where I spent so many heavenly hours, was now a mass of noxious weed with an unhealthy scum on the surface. Further up, near the rapids, I could see (and smell) the clusters of rubbish caught amongst the rocks. I couldn't face a closer examination of it just then.

At supper there was another inquisition.

'Have you thought over what I said?'

'About what?'

'Well, for one, about the local people. They won't accept you.'

'They never did. Except one or two. And no doubt — if they're still alive — will accept me now. Anyway I don't have to go near the village. And I'm sure no one remembers me.'

'There'll be people who'll remember.'

'What, for heaven's sake?'

'The way you behaved. With that fellow Begley.'

So that was it. All those years ago, the one bright star of my surly adolescence. Fishing with Arthur, swimming with him, playing up at the old railway line, flattening halfpennies into pennies. And the kiss. My first one. The one that made me feel as though I had wings, had left the ground, the breath gone out of me.

'Constance said you went overboard.'

I couldn't take any more. That rare time. Buried like a precious artefact. Dug up like shit and thrown into my face. It was obscene. I snapped at him that if Begley called I'd make myself scarce and I went upstairs seething with anger.

You are getting at something, dear brother. Constance said. Constance implied. Constance, Constance.

Reynold was never a child. No innocence of joy for him.

Always adult and sensible was my brother. And a bully with it.

I slept meagrely at night, waking often, longing for dawn.

When eventually I rose I remembered I'd been here a week and nothing had changed between us. Reynold busies himself in and out of town negotiating with saw-millers — for the sale of dying trees — and also does business with the Co-op, where he informed me Begley works as managing director. Also he has bought four Friesian bullocks. I overheard our neighbour say "Some buying in two of them hoors." Which two?

I'm stuck on my wanderings. Some days I've a lot of energy and on others I just want to laze around, let the thoughts take over.

At those times, it seems, I'm not really here. Not fighting to get Reynold to accept me. It's like a prolonged holiday, perhaps. But I'm not bored. Reforming patterns in my head, I suppose. One sliver of success. I've persuaded Reynold to let me do the cooking and the ordering of supplies. We eat well, at last!

I saw the girl again. Caught up with her finally. Like smoke she streaked through the trees and tried to hide.

I called and when she knew she was cornered she turned her back on me but stood still.

I was interested, I don't know why. I felt she was part of the place. Had always been there, like my thoughts, and would escape me forever if I didn't catch her then. I asked her name.

Without turning she said, 'Cathy.'

I had a faint feeling of repugnance, her hunched back was both defiant and cowed.

But I couldn't leave it at that. I asked her down to the house.

'Ah no, miss.'

'Why not?'

'Mister doesn't like me there.'

'How do you know?'

'He saw me once and run me.'

'He's out now. You can come with me.'

She followed carefully, walking like one with the toes curled. At the kitchen door she hovered.

'It's OK.' I was afraid I had trapped something I shouldn't have.

She went in, however, with a sort of bounce, a feeling of achievement, perhaps.

'Sit down.'

'Do you live here?'

I said I thought so. I asked her where she had come from.

'Below. In the Estate.'

I had noticed the 'Estate'. A cluster of local authority dwellings badly planned — over a mile to the shops. No joke when you're straggling along with three or four kids. And the mud. And the rain.

To keep up the chat I asked her how many there were in her family. She told me six and Jim. He had bad blood, she said.

'Bad blood?'

'Me ma took him in.'

'That's hard on you, is it?'

'She gets paid.'

'Are you supposed to mind him?'

She didn't answer. She fidgeted with everything while I made tea and put out some bread and butter, barely sitting on the chair. She wanted cake. I had none so I gave her some of Reynold's precious biscuits. She began stuffing them into her mouth two at a time.

'What's your name?'

'Dilly.'

'Do you have a telly?'

'Only a radio.'

She catechised me at length about all the latest pop stars, none of whose names I knew, and about a local hero called Bud Reilly and was my hair always like this, or was I a witch and how old was I. But the question that still nagged in her head was, did I live here?

Did I? Do I?

I belong here. But am I really in this place that had measured out the formative years of my childhood and adolescence?

And she? The signs of normality were somehow more disturbing. A child of the forest (me?) I wanted. Not this sly urbanised bag of tricks. When she'd eaten she got up and poked around. In and out of cupboards, exclaiming at the jars and packets of different flour and the small pots of herbs I'd brought all the way from London. She took down the radio and fiddled with the knobs till she got some loud rock music. She suddenly came up to me and touched my arm as though to prove I was real. A shiver rode up my spine.

'Dilly!' She laughed — a ripple of scorn. 'That's a funny name.'

I told her she'd have to go soon. That Mister was due back (I could imagine his face if he found her here). She was again standing on a chair poking into the top of the dresser. She jumped down and flew out of the door without a word.

Cathy? Cathy Magee? And what a mess she'd left. I heard Reynold's car before I had time to finish tidying. The radio still blared.

He whirled in and immediately turned off the radio, saying 'What are my biscuits doing on the table?'

'I was looking for a chocolate one.'

'If you want chocolate biscuits you can order them from Mrs Partridge.'

'She must be a hundred if she's a day.'

'It's her daughter-in-law.'

Jack Partridge. Another memory. Acne and mockery. I wondered what self-sacrificing woman had married such a person. Many miles I used to walk to circumnavigate his jeers.

Reynold bustled out but was back in immediately. 'Where's my Philips screwdriver? I left it on the windowsill. Look, Dilly, I wish you wouldn't interfere with my belongings. And my tobacco tin is gone. Where did you put that?'

'I don't touch your things.' Shit, I thought, so it's not only the biscuits I'll have to replace. I pretended to hunt around knowing damn well where they'd gone. I offered him a cigarette, which he snatched, breaking off the filter as though it would bite him.

Earlier, too, I had noticed one of the bullocks trailing a leg. By now I was thoroughly annoyed with myself. What had I started with this Cathy?

I went out into the field. The four bullocks were huddled in the furthest corner. As I approached they began to shuffle nervously and sure enough, one of them limped. Not only limped, but had a piece of wire entangled in its hoof. I'd already walked the length of the field and knew there had been no barbed wire lying about. I cursed out loud.

As the weeks go by I seem to spend much time between the kitchen and the woodshed. Chopping wood and cooking. Not exactly what I came home for. My male chauvinist brother should be enchanted. Should be!

My wanderings in between bring on a fever of planning: new galvanised roofs for the outhouses, rebuilt sheds and walls, a yard full of glossy hens and fresh eggs for sale at twice the village price. Not to mention the old garden, well dug and manured, supplying us with succulent Kerrs Pinks, and every kind of vegetable. But yesterday I rapidly despatched my kitchen chores and, without being aware, made straight for the line of chestnuts.

Cathy was there. When she saw me she began to gather twigs, edging further away without actually running.

Nonchalant, I sat on a branch, stared with indifferent eyes at the profuse weeds round my feet. But my thoughts were not on identifying weeds.

She was gone. Hopped over the fence. Would she return later? I wandered away. Back to the house.

The day went on uneventfully. Uneven of temper, I cleaned shelves, baked bread. Avoided Reynold at supper.

By the river later, I spent a while gazing into the muck. Could no longer resist poking at the rubbish tossing behind the rapids.

A fearful stench rose up when I was foolish enough to release a grey bundle which lay like a muscle behind a large boulder. Sure enough, it was a drowned dog wrapped in a coalsack. Morbidly I dwelt on its slow death as it kicked against its plastic cerements. I slithered on the stones, got soaked, but managed to encourage it over the waterfall whence it hurtled on downstream to the pool in which I used to swim as a child. There the current slowed and the corpse bumped like an abandoned vessel from side to side of the overhung banks.

'Oh keep the dog far hence that's friend to man . . .'

From the line of chestnuts, long-felled stumps have rolled some way down the hill. Layers of fungi, like broken plates, cling to their sides. It was here the following day that we bumped right into each other. While Reynold was out I'd taken the chain saw and planned to cut some of these stumps into manageable logs.

She came barging down the hill as though she wanted to meet me.

After a few non-committal remarks I asked her how come the bullock got tangled in the wire.

'Dunno.'

'Do any of your family come up here?'

'Dunno.'

'Who's Jim?' I tried another tactic.

'I said me ma took him in.'

'Kind of her. Why?'

'His da killed his ma. Ma gets paid.' She was breaking a long stick into little pieces.

A stunner, all right. Like the barbed wire round the bullock's hoof, people leave things lying round deliberately to do harm.

'So you're supposed to mind the young ones?'

'S'right, miss.'

'Dilly.'

'Dilly.' Again that ripple of scorn.

'Did people talk about the place after my father died?'

'Me da said it was a shame.'

'That the place was empty?'

Cathy shrugged and went to break more sticks.

'What else did he say?'

'Said them bloody Prods should be shot.'

'Do you think that, too?'

'Dunno.'

'What does your father do?'

'Nothing. He's on the labour. He gets drunk every night.'

'I see.'

She was climbing the fence — a ramshackle affair of briars with a thin line of wire running through it. Awkward with her bundle of twigs, the thorns jagging at her clothes, and into the inhospitable mud beyond. What a landscape. Stony badly-drained fields, switch-back hills and slopes. But on this summer's day when the sun shone without reservation there was a kind of complacency about everything, even a restored nobility which could not but raise my spirits. And she was gone. Doesn't say cheerio. Just goes.

How quickly I am prey to new obsessions! How foolhardy to imagine space and time might change me. Reynold? How could he, a less malleable animal, be expected to change either?

Two days of silence by no means implied a truce.

Silence forever — a great web of silence would have pleased me.

But everywhere I hid I couldn't escape Cathy's words.

I argued with myself that not everyone was like Cathy's father. He was obviously a drunken wreck whose thoughts must have run on parallel tracks for decades. Still. But it didn't stop me wanting to see her.

Haunted thus, it was I who broke the silence one supper.

'People round here never did accept us, Reynold.'

'You're being morbid.'

'You were away a lot. School. Canada. I knew what people thought. All those years ago. And now, when everything is exaggerated, do you think by some magic they're more tolerant? If father hadn't lorded it around as if he was one of the planter stock — which he wasn't — we might have been accepted within our pitch. But oh no. He wasn't interested. Soon as mother died he and Constance headed off like a couple of lovers. Race meetings, theatres in Dublin, the fields set to an acquisitive neighbour. It was father who could have expanded. It was he who had the money. Look at McDonagh's acres. You wouldn't think they were in the same country. And God knows old McDonagh is not the most energetic man in the world. But ... he keeps his tractor going ... gets in the silo ...'

'Stop raving, Dilly. And once and for all leave Constance out of this. I know my speed. And the sum of my savings. If I keep my nose clean and what's called a "low profile", things will work out.'

God, how logical. God, how insensitive. God, how right you are dear brother. If only I could be invisible.

I shut up thoroughly while wondering how much money he had in the bank.

There followed an awful night.

I tossed and turned. It became a long journey, sometimes with Cathy, sometimes with Reynold. 'Jim' of the bad blood lurked, Cathy's shadow.

When the dawn came I went and stood náked in the bathroom, the bare boards of which shot a chill up my legs. I sponged myself down with lukewarm water and went back to bed hoping to sleep. But it was pointless. Sweat poured off me again.

That way she touches me. Like someone testing the heat of the bathwater. And her home? What of it?

The field in which the houses stood had once been part of our land, but father had been obliged to sell it under a Compulsory Purchase Order. Not that he cared. But I remember how it was. A fine flat field, full of cowslips. We grew hay there for the cows. I could still feel the scratches on my legs as I slid down the haycocks in July. Then, come autumn, there was a crop of blackberries which we kids would pick for hours, filling buckets for the jam, our faces purple from the berries we'd eaten. I cursed myself for this moment of nostalgia. Live not in the past but in the present continuous. Think of it down there — a teeming mass of over-stretched humanity, shouting, drunkenness, valium, yearly pregnancies.

When sleep came at last it was thin. I woke under a buckle of bedclothes, the sun already high.

At breakfast (very late this morning, Dilly) a lecture on Arthur Begley.

'He's a rich man now.'

'Good.'

'Does that not worry you? Make you annoyed?'

'Worry? Annoy? Why?'

'So you don't give a damn about anything.'

'Of course I do. I care most vehemently about certain things. And people.'

'The child?'

I felt the blood leave my face.

Cathy? What can he have found out? On the other hand three was nothing to find out. All, all was in my head. I tried to calm myself.

'What do you mean?' My voice a bare croak.

'The child you might have brought up but didn't.'

'In the name of God?'

'Everyone knew.'

'What are you talking about?'

'Come off it, Dilly. Your habit of lying has surely not persisted to this day? Admit it. Now that so many years have passed. Everyone knew that you left in a hurry because you were going to have Begley's child.'

The letters! That explained it. Father's letters. Attacking but ambiguous. Never mentioned a child but everything else I did was wrong. Eventually I tore them up without reading them. When I used to see his handwriting on the envelope my whole body became still and frozen. Yes, I had to stop reading them to preserve my sanity.

'I don't know what you're talking about.'

'Stop reiterating. How are you going to face him when he calls? It's most embarrassing for me.'

For you, dear brother?

'I'll hide.' The whole matter had now become comical and I burst into peals of laughter. 'Besides,' I said, my chest heaving, 'he won't think he'd made me pregnant . . . I mean . . . you know what I mean.'

'Dilly. Stop that at once. And don't pretend to be ingenuous. You're not a child now.'

'Who started all this? Surely not Constance. She would never have done a thing like that. Why oh why? God, what a scandal then. I can just imagine the village squeezing the last drop out of it.'

'Have it your own way. Even if it can't be proven everyone knew that Dilligence Strong was having an affair with Begley. You were ... an object of much derision.'

'I didn't know. How could I? I was only sixteen. I thought I was in love. I was in love. I thought people in love were allowed to kiss.'

'You're lying. You were always a liar. You have an answer to everything.'

'Oh Reynold, please.'

'Constance said you went overboard.'

I ran from him then. Up the stairs, tears blinding me. In my room with its peeling wallpaper, tatty furnishings, ancient bed, all my energy left me. I stood for maybe hours at the window, only vaguely conscious of the advancing day, or my view of the derelict yard.

I thought often of leaving after that. I crept around like a zombie automatically doing my chores. I even thought of London a lot. Thought of the one man with whom I might have shared my life. How he had begged me not to leave. I remember saying 'But I'm going home,' and he answering 'But this is your home'.

We had spent the last day together. He had a pet mouse which he often took up and stroked. We shared the mouse that day. To pet and fondle. I told him I could share his mouse but not his wife any more.

And yet. Once father had died I knew my destiny. I *had* to come back.

He was Polish. He had come with the last lot of refugees out of Poland in 1944. With his parents who had since died. I tried to explain. I even asked him what he'd do if someone offered him his old home back. But he had no pleasant memories — only air raids and long, long waits at railway stations, his baby brother dying in his mother's arms. He liked London. He had got his degree there and now taught Slavonic Studies in the university.

There was no one else or no other reason for me to go back to London. But I knew it would be crazy to try to pick up the old life. Even after this short time here I knew I could never live in another country again.

But on those dark days I thought about him a lot. I thought only of the good times, naturally. Not the other bad times. How we had to hide, never to be seen together in public. How his wife had threatened suicide several times. He assured me he had never loved his wife, only married her to give her a passport — he himself had become a naturalised Englishman. Nevertheless she had come to depend on him and nothing could eradicate my guilt.

No, I had to stay here, fight to the death, even. I would never go back to him. What about the others? The intermittent lovers and the booze to counterbalance the everpresent shadow of his marriage? Did I want to go back to them or their replacements?

It was with an enormous effort that I fought to get back my reserves of energy. One night, when I was as usual grappling with my insomnia, I sat up in bed and switched on the light. I looked keenly at the cut of my room.

Next morning I ordered wall paint, scrapers, brushes, rollers. The colours would be light and airy, combinations of grey and honey.

After breakfast (for the last while I had refused to eat with Reynold), I walked the fields doing sums. I caught a brief glimpse of Cathy but I didn't call her.

The wind rose. The tall firs claqued and creaked, a distant cow lowed, the bullocks huddled in a clump by the gate. The countryside was moving in preparation for a storm.

That evening I ate again with Reynold but in silence. The wind raged against the window panes and Reynold went round the house closing the shutters. The flames tore up the back of the stove. Every so often puffs of smoke would fill the room and the windows had to be opened again.

We read, watery-eyed, one each side of the table, bodies stiff in their chairs till eventually I could hear his chair being scraped back and the lights on the stair being switched on, then off, his bedroom door closing.

I followed him up and closed my own door softly. I fell asleep with the light on.

Each layer of wallpaper is a division of my childhood. Pink and white roses on a green trellis background, mumps. How the detested Dr McCarthy came with his freezing stethoscope and tactless jokes ('This is how you'll look when you are middle-aged'). (Wrong, I look worse.)

The yellow canary motif. Chickenpox, and later measles. With measles I hallucinated. Constance in the bed beside me. We threw mashed potato on the ceiling.

The paper drops in dollops at my feet. It gathers in a mulch. Every so often I stop and press it into plastic sacks.

Mother beat us for throwing the potato. Reasonable enough.

Worked all day, easing my mind from its monsters, muscles aching, bones creaking. The wall, the plain dull brown wall, emerged. The body of the house was exposed at last.

'What on earth are you at?'

Of course Reynold had to catch me in my paint-stained overalls when I was slinking downstairs for a cup of tea.

'What does it look like?'

'I won't have it.'

'Reynold, whether I go or stay or die in the meantime, paint on the walls and plaster in the holes will improve the value of the property.'

Value, property, use, commodities, resources, viability, all his favourite buzz-words. I'll throw them in his face if he complains about this again.

I refused to talk at supper.

'If,' he began.

'No,' I yelled.

'If ...'

'Oh, go on then.'

'If you worried about the state of the house why didn't you apply yourself to it when father was alive? Come home to keep him company after Constance ... disappeared? He must have been lonely ... Constance after all always kept in touch with him, even when she was working in the North she visited him frequently. Constance ...'

'Was murdered.'

'Dilly.'

'Burnt to death.'

'There is ... was no ... proof ... ever ... their bodies were never found.'

'There's a border between grief and death, Reynold. Accept it now and grieve. Don't keep fighting it. Hoping, like father, that one day she'll walk in the door.'

He was clenching and unclenching his hands. A narrow stream of sweat ran down each side of his brow. A pulse beat clearly in his temples. With extreme cruelty I continued.

'The burning of her house may not be condoned but it must be understood.'

'Don't,' he muttered.

'I hate to upset you like this but if you don't face up to it there's no hope for you. No hope at all.'

Silenced gathered. Embers fell in the stove. We didn't look at each other. Finally he spoke.

'You will never, repeat never, speak to me like that again. Save that talk for your Irish friends in London ... Your ...'

'Shut up, Reynold. Your self-control is torture. Do you not understand what I am trying to say?'

Maybe I should have left it. But I was angry. I knew he deliberately misunderstood me although, God knows, I knew his grief was genuine.

He became very angry.

'Talking like that would have broken father's heart.'

'I daresay.'

'You are appalling.'

'Yes.'

'What do you mean, Yes?'

'What I say. You think I'm appalling. Therefore I am.'

'I can't speak to you any more.'

'Good.'

I was horrified. There I was sitting at a table with a man who had adopted all his father's lines and trying to bargain in a cul-de-sac.

But then. But then. No matter what, half this place is mine.

He still sat, although he appeared quite calm again. I got up and switched on the immersion heater.

'If you're planning a bath remember that the cost of heating the water is twice that of every other electrical device.'

'I'll remember.'

While waiting for the water to heat I stripped the last few feet of wallpaper, cutting into the woodwork round the windows. A crater of plaster, the size of a torso, crumbled away at my feet.

Work makes work, I mourned, swept up the mess and subsided in my bed.

I woke in the dead dark, shuffled downstairs. The water seethed in the boiler. Thank God you're in bed, dear brother, and sleep well and heavily. The loud clip of the switch made me stand still for a minute. But no sound issued from his room. I laughed myself into the bath.

It took me a long time to clean between my toes. Under my jeans I have shapely legs. I coursed over the other spaces and folds that go to make up the female body and a brown scum gathered.

Since starting on my room I notice nothing except scratched paint, dog-eared wallpaper, greasy surfaces. Have I the energy to meet the future even half-way? God knows what woodworm, dry rot, loosening plaster, ceiling cracks, I'll encounter on my journey. I lie back in the water dreaming of a perfectly renewed house, knowing that once round, I'd have to start all over again.

The soothing therapy of painting and patching was interrupted one afternoon by the arrival of a foreign car in the yard. That is to say, it had a different engine noise from Reynold's. Who was it only Begley, my alleged seducer.

Forgetting my promises to hide, I ran down the stairs and into the yard. But instead of greeting me with open arms he said, 'Is your husband in?'

'No ... er, no. His car's gone. He must be in the village.'

'Will you ask him to drop down to my office? I'm Begley. Arthur Begley.'

You are indeed, Arthur Begley. I gazed him up and down. Had I changed so drastically?

'He knows where to find me.'

He didn't go, however, but remained in the driver's seat, one hand on the open door, one foot in the gravel. 'What do you think of the place?'

'Lovely.'

'Not much doing in the way of social life.'

'I don't mind.'

(If I cut out the eyes, lashes — long healthy black lashes — eyes also clear with brass flecks — I could throw away the rest of him.)

The lanky lad with big feet, the narrow face, the dark sunburnt skin, the hollow cheeks, the brick-red lips, cut like a kiss, had all gone. They had given place to this all-in-one person.

'I'd ask you in, only I'm up to my neck in decorating a room.' My laugh made him look at me. Perhaps only my laugh hadn't changed.

'I wouldn't want to bother you.' Those eyes!

I wished my hands would stop shaking.

'Pity your father-in-law let the place get so run down. He could have broken even at least. But he'd rather set the land than farm it. Can't blame him, I suppose — living here on his own. Dempsey bought a lot. But your old man didn't understand business seemingly. Of course five or six years ago it was different. There were grants and bank loans for everything. If you blew your nose itself they'd grant you a dozen handkerchiefs. Joking aside, though, I'd say your husband has his head screwed on.'

I looked at him long and hard. He had plucked success out of the lean years — the fifties and early sixties. Apart from running the Co-op he has a large farm on both sides of the border some five miles from Morecleath. Yes. When nearly all our generation took the boat he'd had the sense to stay. Sensible. Had it made him sensible?

'Not much trouble around these parts recently,' I probed.

'Sure we're all the one, aren't we?'

'That's not what I asked, but never mind.'

'You know how it is. We're all on friendly terms. Each lot keeps their views to themselves.'

Gently, but gently, he was telling me to shut up.

Still he lingered. Offering me scraps of information about the neighbours and ending with, 'Your father-in-law was a nice-spoken man.'

'He was arrogant. He could destroy people like salt destroys slugs.'

'Strong way to put it.'

'Not far from the truth.'

'Trouble was, he was too much drawn to the city. A bit wasteful of the place. Not good to see that. After the children left it was lonely. Surprising he never married again. Fine cut of a màn, carried his age well. He didn't mix much with the local people. Reckon he was shy, not many of his kind left to talk to.'

'To hell with it.'

'Pardon?'

'To hell with it. He was a snob. He had nothing to be snobbish about. His father was a businessman with a penchant for long odds. Which came off. Surprisingly. So my father ... in law, wanted to become an old-fashioned gentleman overnight.'

'Not much love lost between the two of you.' Oh, the little wrinkles round the eyes, the long eyelashes. 'I'd say "young" Mr Strong would be more of the business type.'

'Yes, as you call him "young" Mr Strong has his head screwed on ... Did you not meet him down the years when he used to visit his father?'

'Can't say I did. Not since the daughters left anyway.'

Did he look at me curiously? I'm not sure.

'Everyone knows everyone, don't they?'

'Hard not to.'

Once you stuffed sloes in my mouth and I spat them out in your face. And your sharp look of anger. I had wanted to cry but didn't dare because for a moment I realised it was possible you despised me for my background, for the privileges you assumed I had. Perhaps the roles are reversed now. The balance redressed. But who knows. There are sure to be other drunken Mr Magees like Cathy's father. I wanted to ask about her family but was afraid I might rake up a nest of slugs.

He told me there were new Protestant farmers from across the border a few miles away. 'Came in shortly after the Troubles and bought old McGivern's place. He'd let the land get sour. They paid good money too, hard cash. You need a lot. There's people thinks all farmers have it easy now. Not so. The banks own everything. Come day go day. But there's plenty of spending. Not like in the old days.'

And I had to ask, 'Are you married?'

'Well and truly, worst luck.'

'Not that bad, surely?'

'It's worse for her. Kids make you a bit cynical. You're never done with them and you wouldn't be without them. Even when they're grown up.'

'Nice to have met you.' I held out my hand, afraid to say more.

As he drove away, scattering stones under his wheels, I felt the mutilation of years lie heavy on me.

Back at work the damp and devastation was overpowering. I attacked the walls like an enemy.

At supper the message delivered caused in turn the clutching of the hair, the swivelling on the chair as though he were about to throw himself on an approaching thug, with, 'I knew it, I knew it.'

My previous day's cruelty, my temerity, had left no mark. My dear brother does not stay on the defensive for long.

'He didn't recognise me.'

'Look, Dilly, this is embarrassing. Who did he think you were, then?'

'Your wife.'

'My wife? You idiot. Everyone knows I'm a widower. Now they'll think you're my mistress.'

'So what?'

'It's not funny. Don't you understand anything?'

Only too well, dear brother.

'It is funny. You must admit it.'

'Dilly!'

Poor Reynold. Swivelling and fuming because his precious reputation is at stake. He talked about getting in touch with Mr Forbes.

'For a divorce?'

'Dilly!'

'Well, you can't change father's will now.'

'Maybe we could prove something about father's state of mind. Because of Constance's disappearance.'

'Do me out of my share? Do you mean that?'

'Of course not. You'd be properly financed, we'd see to that.'

I left him with these optimistic meanderings to go back to my decorating.

Honey. Yes, the colour works well. One wall done and already the room looks more hospitable.

How diligent I was! I took a few hours off to sort out old books. One caught my eye and I got stuck into it at once.

Reynold, home after shopping, burdened with parcels, unleashed himself.

'Look,' I said, waving the book at him, *Progressive Farming for the Small Man*. A few useful hints. Listen.' I threw the shop bread — which he insists on buying — into the bin. Reynold leaned back in his chair, sniffed over his moustache.

'"While recultivating the land it is advisable to adopt some measure of insurance as you wait for the soil to mature. Pig farming in a small way is the most obvious outlet and one with the minimum risk. Well-drained sties can be erected out of old farm buildings in a very short time with little expense . . ." etc. So, would you trust me to set up in pigs? They advise a dozen or so bonhams to start with.' I showed him the diagram. 'Look. It shows you how to set about the drainage and what's called a simple French drain can be quickly dug.'

He pushed the book away.

'One of your trendy writers. The sort of thing I imagined you'd go for. Greenpeace-back-to-the-land. Quite unreal. Do it yourself rubbish and starve later . . ."

'Don't be absurd. This is nothing like what you describe.'

Reynold laughed loudly and scornfully. 'One of father's, then, which he occasionally picked up imagining he'd get the place back on its feet.'

'He was a great one for interior innovations — didn't he design the plumbing?'

We were both laughing now. Was Reynold melting? My heart rose.

'The retired city gent — wouldn't sully his hands with buying and selling,' I continued. A mistake. The normal cloud settled back over Reynold's face.

'How do you know? You hadn't lived with him for years.'

'I knew him well. I lived with him for the first sixteen and a half years of my life, didn't I? There's nothing I don't know about father.'

'If you were so concerned why didn't you come to his funeral?'

'I never said I was concerned about him. Knowing a person

doesn't make you like him, does it?' I gave him a hard look as I prepared to start cooking the supper.

'Sit down, Dilly. We'll have it out once and for all.'

We?

'Have what out?'

'What happened while I was in Canada?'

'Nothing. I left home.'

'Why did you leave?'

'I got a job through an agent in Dublin. A job in Birmingham. In an aircraft factory. So I left. Constance was in charge. She was going to college in Dublin, came home every weekend and then they went off carousing. I didn't fancy being a skivvy all my life to a man who disliked me so intensely.'

'You exaggerate. You were never treated badly.'

'What do you know?' I felt my gut contracting. 'And not content with getting rid of me he wrote me terrible letters. Laughed at me. Said I imagined I was fighting for the rights of small nations and what I did wouldn't make a ha'porth of difference. My duty was to my own small nation. Him, in other words. What did he care about Ireland? When de Valera asked everyone to grow food, what did he do? Set the land. He tried to order me back to cook and clean for both of them. I wouldn't come.'

'It was your duty!'

'To a mud-slinging parent who wouldn't even let me go to college? There were loads of Irish girls working over there alongside me in the factory. They were all Catholic girls, ostensibly from narrow-minded families. They never got letters like I did. They'd get friendly supportive letters, parcels of butter and bacon. I never got so much as a ten-shilling note. And there was no cause for his fury. I supported myself, asked nothing of him. He could afford a housekeeper. As time passed I grew less sensitive to his attacks. Eventually I didn't read his letters. Then when Constance got married she wrote and asked me would I consider returning. I didn't answer that letter.'

'Leave Constance out of it once and for all. I loved her.'

'So did I.'

Like two galloping horses in a dray we pulled up simultaneously. I glimpsed my face in the mirror. My round blue eyes had a frightened look in them. Why was that? I didn't feel frightened, merely frustrated. But perhaps I was. Frightened of the power of death. His eyes are just like mine. The only feature we have in common. I'm long and lean. He's stocky. My head is too big for my body. His is neat and fits the rest of him. His hands are small in comparison to mine. My hands are large, square, workworn from scraping old furniture and polishing it up for sale in my junk shop. His back is square, the back of a man who has pored over papers all his life. Mine is narrow, slightly hollow, like a question mark.

We sat there, the same genetic patterns of blood and growth, both thinking of our sister, who — to me at least — seems to be the one who has caused this unbridgeable gap.

There must be a moment when the hand is held out and taken. Even the hangman must long to take the hand of the man who is sentenced to die. But how to recognise and capture that moment?

His crisp, 'So you admit it,' scattered these thoughts like a gunshot scatters crows.

'Admit what?' my voice was barely audible.

'That you went over there to have Begley's child.'

'God. Must we go into all that again?'

'Once and for all.'

'I will not. I will not admit to having his child. Begley's or anyone else's. You're trying to pin some crime on me as an excuse to get me out of here. And even if it were true what relevance does it have to our sharing the work here today? Why are we fighting? Fighting about dead people and people who were probably never born. Who can't answer for themselves. Father was a fair man but he wasn't human. He was fair, that is, to me in his will. I'd like to think you are. Perhaps you are. At least you voice your hatred of me like mother did. I was never in any doubt about mother's hatred of me. I wasn't a boy, for one.'

'Dilly!'

'No. You asked for it. To have it out once and for all.'

'I only asked.'

'No. Do you see this scar?' Reynold made a face as though someone had defecated in front of him. 'Exactly. Disgusting, isn' it? Makes my face lopsided. Well, who was responsible for that?'

'We all know the story.' He shuffled his hands over his papers.

'All right. Tell me then.'

'You, er ... fell off your bicycle or something.'

'Or something. Half my face was hanging off and all I got was abuse. And was it stitched up? No. They wouldn't send me to the hospital because they said it would teach me a lesson. Right. Enough about that. But to go back to these grossly neglected acres, bog, drumlins, stony, leaking, why the bloody hell don't you let me do the donkey work? For God's sake, man, listen to me. Let me start my small pig unit which would feed us both.

Give you time. You seem to think all this rehabilitation can be done in a year. I can drive a tractor. I'm not afraid of rubber boots and muck ... you accuse me me of being a romantic ... but what about you? You'd need a hundred thousand pounds saved if you want to speed up. Can we not go step by step?' I had to stop. He was holding his head in his hands as though he was feeling real pain.

'Leave it,' he muttered.

He sat back, picked up his knife and fork. But his dinner had gone cold. He pushed his hands forward, wrists resting on the edge of the table. Surveyed his food, me, the stove, said coldly, 'My daughter Deirdre and her husband and child are coming for the weekend. They'll sleep in Constance's old room.'

It was all in all a successful weekend. Reynold's daughter exhumes a side of him that he carefully hides from the world. She treats him like an old-fashioned, lovable eccentric. She bosses him like she bosses her husband and child.

However, to describe her character without being bitchy myself I'll just have to record the conversation I overheard when they arrived. (They swept up the drive as if shock absorbers and track rods were two a penny. They have a smart Japanese limousine which she drives. Her husband, Gerald, seems to do most of the baby-minding. He was sitting in the back with his son, an infant of some four years.)

Up to my neck in wall paint at the open window I was at an excellent vantage point to eavesdrop on their greetings. After the recognised familial hugs Reynold declared that he had bad news.

'Dilly's turned up.'

'It was on the cards. Aunty Dilly. Well, well. I thought she hated the place.'

'Apparently not. She seems to have been hankering after it all these years or something. It's unfortunate.'

'What does she look like?'

'Terrible.'

'How do you mean? I know she always looked weird. Is she bald or something?'

'Anything but. She has far too much hair. Just awful. Her whole person is an embarrassment. You'll see her at tea.'

'Has she brought a man with her?'

'No, thank God.'

'Oh father, I do love you so. You are so old-fashioned.'

'Thanks. Will I fetch Jonathon out of the car?'

'God, no. Let sleeping dogs lie. He was really bad-tempered till he dropped off about ten minutes ago.'

'I'll put on the kettle. I have biscuits for the little fellow.'

I slid out of my overalls thinking of the cake I'd baked for them — fuck them for a lousy lot — anyway what did I expect? That he announce my presence with joy?

On my way into the sittingroom Reynold and I passed each other like two cars on a narrow road.

He had lit the fire and dusted the surfaces, so now they were savouring the fruits of his toil by standing decoratively one each side of the mantelpiece. A spear of sunlight made the room look really shabby. Faded chintzes, a once decent carpet threadbare and stained near the fireplace. By contrast, the young husband and wife looked fit and fashionable.

I extended a hand to both of them.

Deirdre is a tall dark-browed woman; a nose which is sometimes called Roman dominates her face. She was wearing dark red lipstick which worked well with her out-of-doors complexion. (I gather she is keen on mountaineering and goes climbing every weekend.) She is heavy-bosomed and narrow-waisted with a small rib-cage and with her hair parted in the middle and held back with a tortoiseshell comb. By and large she would be very nearly a beauty of a mid-Victorian type.

'Hullo, Aunty Dilly.' She laughed hum-hym-hum.

'Please call me Dilly. Drop the aunt.'

'You've come to stay, I believe. You must be mad. Who'd want to stay in a place like this? All the people round here seem to be a dull crew.'

'You call us all "culchies", I suppose. What's so great about town people anyway?' Did I catch a smile from Gerald? 'It depends a lot on what you want from the rural community.' I had to continue with inane generalisations in order to keep up the chat, propounding on how all blow-ins are suspect — for years even — and ending with, 'I wonder does Reynold realise quite what type of suspicion he's up against.'

'Who'd be suspicious about father? Poor old father's so straight no one could be suspicious of him.'

Another smile from Gerald?

This is a shrewd one, this Deirdre. Practical, selfish, utterly satisfied with her lot.

'What sort of suspicion are you talking about anyway?'

Was she getting interested? But did I really have to explain?

'I grew up here, don't forget. Long before the current troubles began. In my day — as a child — smuggling was the name of the game. They used to cycle the white bread over the border and tea and sugar and bicycle tubes. But large as life the differences underneath. I was acutely aware of this as a child. The gallop of capitalism OK. Cowboy landlords in the cities OK. So long as their lip service goes to the parish priest.'

'Heavens above, Aunty Dilly, you're raving. We just live our lives how we like in Dublin. No one takes a blind bit of notice whether you go to church or not. You're living in the past. Do you hear me, Gerald?'

'Oh well, let's not be too heavy about it. I've baked a cake which I hope will sweeten everyone's nature.'

Deirdre hum-hymmed and Gerald fiddled with the photos of Constance on the mantelpiece.

I looked into her strong arrogant eyes. Petrol pure. Brighter than her father's. Sharp. Was I supposed to tell her about the 'pull of roots', sample her cynicism, have her tell me how easy life is if you shut your eyes and steer a middle course (added, of course, to your decent house, reasonable husband, au-pair girl and Japanese limousine)? But ... mountaineers are strange animals. Never satisfied. They crave for greater and greater heights. A Sagittarian complex. Sometimes they overdo it and fall off the back of the Matterhorn! But no. I imagined that even in her mountaineering she would be moderate.

I excused myself and went to the kitchen.

'What a nutter, all right.'

'So that's the terrible aunt.'

I took Jonathon down to the river, made up stories for him. A decent kid. While we sat and dangled our legs I saw Cathy. For nearly a week I hadn't spoken to her. What with Arthur Begley, my maniacal painting, and the diurnal inquisition I had shelved my primordial interest in her. But seeing her suddenly, when I had the child with me, made me uneasy. I felt my pulse quicken. 'Cathy,' I called.

She was at the other end of the field, pretending, as always to have some other interest. She hesitated but came slowly, in the lanky semi-sideways movement she adopts when nervous. 'Come and sit with us. How's things?'

She didn't answer, just stared at Jonathon.

'This is my nephew, Jonathon.'

For a second or two she stood till, with a sudden lunge, she gave him a shove and he all but toppled into the water. He got his socks and shoes wet and started to yowl.

'It's all right. Don't cry. She didn't mean it.' I kept looking at her while I removed the offending garments, holding him on my knee.

Defiant laughter was what I expected but on the contrary her expression was one of remoteness as if the person who had pushed the child was someone different.

Jonathon scrambled off my knee, pleased now to have his feet free, and began to squelch them in the mud at the edge of the bank. I watched anxiously, expecting another schizoid action on her part, but now that the child had moved away she suddenly sat down beside me. I could feel the warmth of her thin bones riding against my thigh.

She hadn't spoken a word, I realised.

'Where have you been lately?'

'Dunno.'

'You must know, Cathy?'

'Me da shut me in.'

We sat silently for a while and then, as I had tried to entertain Jonathon with stories, I told her how the river had once been when I was small. About the dragonflies and otters, and how you could see the trout idling under the stones, the water was so clear. Also how I used to swim in the pool which was now overgrown and murky. She said she couldn't swim. I said I would teach her next week when the family had gone. The stiffness began to leave her. We could have sat on for longer only the child began to whinge for his tea. He wouldn't walk barefoot so I had to pick him up. As soon as I did so her face darkened.

'Will you give it a try?'

'What?'

'A swimming lesson. On Monday?'

'Dunno.' She was edging away. I watched her loping over the clumps of bad grass like an indecisive hare. I turned and carried Jonathon back to the house.

In the yard we paused at the buttock of the broken wall. Deirdre was in the kitchen with Reynold. Her confident voice rang out.

'Do tell, was there an awful scandal? Oh father, how meaty. And do the villager know the evil one has returned?'

'Poor Constance got the worst of it. Everyone loved Constance. They felt sorry for what she had to put up with. Dilly was always impossible, secretive, bad-tempered, but worst of all utterly unable to tell the truth...'

I felt myself closing my fist over Jonathon's shoulder, sweat gathered under my armpits, on my brow. It was with difficulty that I unfroze my face as I entered the kitchen, shoving the child, wet socks and shoes in his hand, in front of me.

'Your cake smells good, Aunty Dilly,' said Deirdre, as though she had been praising me.

Having delivered the child I turned on my heel without answering.

Fighting the cramps in my stomach — muscular knot — I climbed up on my ladder and started 'cutting in'. When a knock came half an hour later, I exploded. 'Jesus, yes?'

'I'm disturbing you.'

Gerald looked up at me, a shy smile on his city face.

'I'd like to apologise.'

'No, please. You've done nothing.'

'I've studied behaviourism amongst the higher primates, but this!' He waved his arm in an arc. 'That! An amalgam of ... deliberate ... well ... why do you take it?'

'Siblings,' I muttered, climbing down, pulling the elastic band off my hair and letting it drop heavily on my shoulders.

'You've wonderful hair.'

'I'm an old woman in a hurry.'

'You'll never be old.'

'Is that what's wrong? Is that bad?'

'No.'

He took the paintbrush from me.

'And thank you for looking after Jonathon. He took a shine to you.'

'In spite of his wet feet?'

The knot in my stomach loosened, the pain left me.

'All in a day's work.'

'It must have been wonderful to grow up here. I'd have loved it. I grew up in the suburbs — Clontarf — nervous mother. Father was a bacon exporter.'

'Sounds like money.'

'Enough to educate me and my brothers.'

'My generation took the boat.'

'We just scraped in between. Lucky.'

'Maybe. I considered myself lucky. There were jobs then. I got my education in Paddington lending library.'

'Yes. Perhaps you're lucky now. Things need doing here. I sit all day in my glasshouse of an office writing reports. I'm miles away from the ground.'

'There's plenty of that around these parts! Still ... it's the reason for my return. I used to spend all day scraping paint off solid Edwardian and Victorian furniture to screw the public out of a few shillings. You know. This craze for clean wood. Old farmhouse furniture and so on.'

'And you're still doing it! Am I keeping you from it?'

'Please don't go. I want to explain something.'

What? Cathy's deliberate action? I wanted to talk about her to someone.

'The child — well — she's around fourteen. Half child, half grown up.'

'You make her sound like a centaur.'

'No. That was a proud creature. This one's feral, all right, but also a waif. She delib ... in a way she was responsible for your son's getting his feet wet. Deirdre will have blamed me.'

'You mustn't take Deirdre seriously.'

'Oh, it's not her blaming me that matters either. Cathy is...' Well, what is she? Neglected, overburdened, sly? Getting at me? To get my attention? Possibly ... Psychiatrists are often wrong.

'It's a mistake to read too deep into things. Gets you into too many difficulties yourself.'

'If I were more secure here, yes.'

'So many complexities and subtleties of character have to be hidden. It makes you angry having to fight on such a narrow ledge.'

'I'm no Spartan!'

'Neither am I!'

His full smile made his rather ordinary face quicken.

So. I told Gerald nothing so as he would understand. I oversay to Reynold. But there's no other way to talk to him.

I was glad when they went and things resumed their colourless indistinction.

There is a short wood of conifers that blinds the eastern side of our farm. She was there, idling.

'Cathy, you got me into trouble yesterday.'

The pine needles crackled under her feet like newspaper.

'Stop walking and listen.'

The habit of days and nights always on the watch for predators, like the watching of the hare, the body trembling, ready to break, made me blunder towards her, compelled to catch her arm.

'Cathy. I'm on your side!' Statement flat and meaningless.

We sat then, on a fallen branch, she near, the bones beneath the flesh brittle as a rabbit's. I pulled her body into mine, I stroked her bare arm beneath the torn jumper. I bent and kissed the hollow in the back of her neck. Skin like india-rubber against my lips. She shrank into the curve of my body.

'Will Mister let you stay?' she whispered this. Her intuition silenced me. She burrowed her hand under my armpit, snuggling her chin between my breasts. 'You won't go, will you?' her voice muffled by the wool of my jumper.

Rabbit bones.

'You will always be here?' she pressed on.

What could I say?

'Rabbit bones,' I muttered.

For a short while she could accept this, but other days when I helped her to gather sticks or she helped me to fill a hole in a gap, she'd sulk for periods of up to an hour which irritated me beyond belief. Or she'd quarrel with me when I had to leave her to attend to my chores, calling me a fucking old bitch. Occasionally she harked back to Jonathon saying, 'He's not much'.

I'd like to say that Cathy is beautiful, gifted, cut out for greater things than being surrogate mother, petty thief. But in truth I cannot. She can barely read and write, having left school the previous year, she has scratchy hair, rather a large face with overwide nostrils, round eyes buried under the bridge of her nose, pale eyebrows and concave cheeks. Not that she is retarded in any way. I once asked her had she no friends of her own age and she said they were all stupid. I tried to interest her in matters of the mind, telling her stories of Greek or Irish heroes, but she'd soon lose interest and sidle off.

At these times I'd wish that I'd never met her, she was an albatross round my neck. I always seemed to be thinking of her when I should have been thinking of Local Authority Grants, Work Programmes, Employment Schemes, in other words help and/or money for restoring the land — that is, the part that interested me and that Reynold ignored — the refurbishing of the yard, the digging of the garden, the planting of vegetables.

I cursed myself for being so profligate all those years. Another would have saved and saved for this very purpose. Oh no. Not me, Dilligence. I spent all my money on ruffians and scroungers and booze as if there were no tomorrow. But. Was I fooling myself? If he — I say his name now — Zoltan — had been able to marry me or at least settle down with me, would I have stayed? That time we had planned to marry, the date, the time, the place, the clothes. But then? His wife withdrew her agreement for a divorce and I said goodbye. No more love. No more sex.

And then my mind would go back to the problem of Cathy. Although I felt no sexual urge for her I appeared obsessed. What the fuck was I at?

I voiced one of my work projects one supper, adding that a

compromise must be found, battles are lost in advance if you put human beings first. So I must approach the situation from both our points of view and from that of the land we were trying to nurture.

He accused me of indulging in metaphysical nonsense and he suggested (again) that he should get a mortgage and give me a share in cash. Then I could buy myself a cottage 'with roses round the door'.

I lost my temper and told him I didn't want a fucking cottage. 'I want this place. My place. The only place I was ever alone in and understood. Simply my place.' Near hysterics, I was. 'I was never able to visit here in the last thirty-odd years. That's a long wait, Reynold. You can't imagine how I felt when I heard from Mr Forbes. I really thought that you'd be only too glad to be shut of the goddamn farm and I could gradually buy you out. But seeing as you are taking it seriously let's tackle the problem at its roots. I'll take the yard and the garden and you take the fields and we'll work separately at our various projects. Can we not come to some agreement like that, stop arguing over every little thing? Or do you want to cut it in half and build a Berlin wall down the middle?'

Of course he couldn't give an inch. He informed me that I knew nothing of modern farming methods (true, but I'm a fast learner) and he rudely hinted that I saw Ireland as a country of shebeens and crocks of gold. As if I were some blue-rinse from across the Atlantic come home to find my l'il ol' cabin. He dismissed me for an urban ingenue which I certainly was not. Complacent bollocks.

So there's no such thing as farming any more. It's agri-business. We don't grow oats to feed the farm animals. We grow barley for the breweries, wheat for Europe, butter for some distant butter mountain. The land isn't poor, medium or good. It's either viable or not. No hens, no spuds, no vegetables, no cheese-making. No home-made bread. Supermarket frozen food in the deep freeze. (Which reminded me we needed a fridge.) Milk from the Co-op. Processed, cling-wrapped life. At least in the cities there are health food shops and lots of us make our own bread. So here in this time-worn, wind-worn, damp part of the world we have to work our brains out to make the damn place viable. As if there were no such thing as a thistle or an artichoke, rain or drought, snow or frost, muscles or aching backs. Shit! Why don't I just pack my bags, I ask myself for the nth time. It'll soon be winter and everything will drip and I'll get bronchitis. But I won't be bored. By God, I won't.

My room is finished at last. No brush-marks, blobs on the ceiling, bubbles under my plaster-work. My brush hand itches to continue round the house. But nearer to thee, dear brother, the further I get from propitiating you.

Yesterday was dramatic. While scrubbing the last few spots off the floor-boards the sound of a car made me peer from the window.

Arthur Begley was already standing on the cobbles looking round with an almost possessive expression. For a frozen moment I wondered if Reynold had negotiated some deal with him. Sold the place from under my feet. I tried to improve my appearance by sponging my eyes with cold water and combing my hair.

'You're out of luck again. Reynold's in town.'

'I haven't come to see him. It's you I've come to see.'

'Arthur. I'm supposed to be incognito.'

'I knew it. I knew.' Absurd gaiety bubbled between us. 'It was when you laughed.'

'Why didn't you say?'

'I still wasn't a hundred per cent sure.'

'Did you not know Reynold was a widower?'

'Well, you know, these things are delicate. You could have been, well. . .'

'His current mistress?' I laughed and laughed, remembering Reynold's alarm at the notion.

'One has no control over village curiosity. I suppose it leaked out.'

I felt then that I would have liked everything to pile up and be taken away by the refuse truck, my guilt, my despair, my memories, to be replaced purely and simply by events. For the first time I felt a surge of optimism.

'I was puzzled all the time. Why I stayed so long, I suppose. But you were out of context. Would you have recognised me if I'd walked into your house in London?'

A fair question.

'I used to picture you as very smart, living the high life, a person who'd never bother to return to this neck of the woods. Who'd find nothing in common with the likes of us any more.'

'And here I am, unsmart, greying, uglier than ever.'

'Don't put yourself down. I'm no oil painting myself.'

To get away from this tactless topic I said I'd wanted to ask him about his father.

Well I remembered him. Gaunt, handsome as a pirate. A farrier who made wrought iron gates and firedogs in his spare time. Eventually he was taken up by the local 'gentry' and they organised a stand for him in the Dublin Spring Show. There under a specially constructed awning for his furnace chimney the crowd paused and marvelled at this great nineteenth century figure, firing, twisting, fashioning, thrusting his tongs into the flames fanned by his enormous bellows.

He grew rich, sent his sons to college, his daughters to be nurses, bought a fine house up the top of the village and drank himself eventually into ruin.

'Is he alive still?'

'He died only two years ago. Eighty-five years old and still as sharp as a blade. A devil of a man. His energy killed my mother, luckily, before she had to watch his financial decline. Ach, we were in the way of keeping ourselves then so we threw him the odd few bob.'

'More than the odd few, I'd say.'

Arthur was smiling in the way of a man remembering a famous stallion or some international monument that's been felled.

Often, as a child, I had dodged underneath the legs of the cart-horses or helped him to hold them. He always wore a khaki shirt rolled up to the elbows. I never saw him in an overcoat, even on the coldest winter's day. Some days he'd give me sweets and on others he'd run me.

'I think your mother bought his first pair of firedogs.'

'Yes. And they're still here.'

We didn't speak of our childhood games while we sat out on the broken wall getting the full heat of the sun. I brought out a tray of tea and scones I'd recently baked. Jam fell on our laps. We drank copiously.

He spoke of his grown children, a son graduated from Agricultural College (mad about organic farming. Should meet Reynold!) Another son running a rock band. His youngest — a daughter — studying biochemistry at Galway University.

'So you were in no jet set?'

I felt a stir of pleasure. So he had actually remembered me from time to time. Sadly, all those years I had seldom given him a thought.

He promised to shop around for bonhams for me — he'd out-crook that crook McDonagh — and I reminded him that I was not a millionaire.

'Reluctantly I must go,' he got up. I was glad to see that he was a little stiff, a trifle overweight — the cards are not all stacked against me!

'Mind your shock absorbers,' I said as I shut him into his car.

'Everything's fine.' His full smile broadened his face, speedy little wrinkles crowded his mouth and eyes. The long eyelashes waved like hands as he backed his car first and then headed off down the avenue.

Of course there was supper to face. I knew I had to inform Reynold that Arthur had called even though I was slitting my own throat. He was bound to find out sooner or later. He was adding figures in his ledger.

'That's three hundred and fifty plus vat.'

'Arthur called.'

'Arthur who?'

'Begley.'

He went rigid like one starting a fit.

'It's not that bad.'

'Well, what have you to say? Now everyone knows in the village that you're back?'

'Strange that no one has called the League of Decency to have me thrown out.'

'Dilly.' He had half swivelled his chair, his two hands holding the edge of the table as if it were a jetty and he was standing in a boat.

'Please, Reynold, don't repeat what you think father would have said.'

'So you flaunted yourself in front of him, I suppose.'

'This tidal wave will only drown yourself, Reynold.'

He went back to his ledger, head down, with a big shrug like a horse throwing its rider.

'You go your way. There's no stopping you.'

I spooned his dinner on to his plate and put it down beside him.

I hope it chokes you, dear brother.

I flounced out of the room, but was shortly back, too hungry to ignore my supper.

He took his glasses out of his pocket and wiped them, holding each lens against the light and, from the centre of his ledger, he took a letter.

When he had carefully donned his spectacles he opened the envelope and began to read.

'Oh my God!' He turned the letter back and read it over.

'Very inconvenient. Very upsetting.'

'Is someone ill?' I enquired.

'Not at all.'

I waited, eating as quickly as possible.

'Dilly!' I looked up.

'Deirdre wants you to look after Jonathon this weekend.'

'I suppose I could.'

'I thought you loved children.'

'What put that idea into your head?'

'You spent a lot of time with him when he was here.'

'Are you accusing me of malpractice?'

'No. We all thought it a bit strange.'

'You had a lengthy discussion about it?' Anger contracted my stomach.

'Not at all.'

'Oh, forget it. Yes, I'll mind him. He can help me with the hen-house.'

'I hadn't planned on keeping hens.'

'Well, I have. A dozen pullets for a start. Don't make it into a crisis. I just want some free-range eggs.'

'Have you any idea what the feedstuff costs?'

'You've asked me that before. It'll balance off against what we spend on stale eggs from the supermarket.' I got up and cleared away the plates. 'I'll go up and get his room ready.'

He was delivered that Saturday, complete with toys and teddy bear.

'Further and further in ... last week pigs ... this week hens. She'll have great sickly birds bringing in God knows what kind of fowl pest. Soon as I get the Well field sown she'll let them straggle all over it and demolish the seed...'

'Poor father. Cheer up.'

Poor dear brother, cheer up. Such misery you endure at my hands.

Deirdre didn't waste time. A sweeping U-turn and she was gone, bouncing down the avenue and sending back a fog of dust like an old-fashioned stage coach.

Jonathon howled till Reynold picked him up and brought him in to me.

'Go to your aunt, young man.' He slapped a kiss on the child as he handed him over.

Saddled with the child I began my attack on one of the more promising outhouses.

'Where is Aunty Constance?'

'She went away to ... she went away.'

'She went where, Aunty Dilly?'

'The north.'

'This is the north.'

'Yes I know. Further north.'

'Is that the North Pole?'

'Not quite that far.'

'Where is she now?'

'She's ... I don't know ... dead.'

'What did she die of?'

'She was ... she just died.'

'I'm going to heaven when I die.'

'Good.'

'Are you going to die soon?'

'A good question.'

'You are very old.'

'A mighty age, all right.'

'I can count up to a hundred.' He proceeded to do so.

Jonathon has a nose like his mother and a mouth like his father. He has a constructive walk. In boxy sweater and rolled-up jeans he forges around in and out while I work, humming up and down the scale like a bee in a flower.

I was making perches and nesting boxes. I made him bring me things to keep him busy. Suddenly she was there. Peering in the door. Full of anger and hurt.

'Cathy, come in. Would you like to help?'

'Why is he here?'

'Oh Cathy, it's not the end of the world. He's only here another day. And you know, "mister" is in the house. He may come out any moment.' Her fury sparked off her. 'Cathy, come here.' She wouldn't budge. 'Where's the child gone?' I felt panic rising in me. She didn't answer but backed out of the coop. Hurriedly I followed but she was round the side. A few minutes later there was an agonised yowling and Reynold came flying out of the house. But Jonathon had merely fallen and cut his hand. Cathy was nowhere to be seen.

Reynold, however, while scooping up the child glared at me with a face full of scorn.

'I thought you were looking after the child.'

There was no point in answering. I just went back to my work. I could see the child snuggling his nose into his grandfather's neck.

Poor Reynold. He has a silent satisfaction in his grandson. Perhaps they chat like old men, exchanging oft-repeated stories, and when silence overtakes them will sit content in each other's company.

My mother hated onions. If a knife had cut an onion and later was used to cut something she was eating, her anger and fear would seethe to the surface. So there was a place for onions. A special place with shelves built off the kitchen. This room would be the right place for my hen food and sacks of wood shavings. To get there I had to pass through the larder — a cool forgotten room of whitewashed stone and wide-flagged floor.

Sometimes I went in there to marvel at a spider. That day, I noticed, the web had gone full circle at last. The spider had stretched her delicate weavings from shelf to shelf and there she was, the tiny mamillae twirling and twisting, never satisfied with her work.

The spinsters and the knitters in the sun
Did used to chaunt it.

This unused room has a smell like cider left at the bottom of a bottle. At one end the ancient disused churn, at a jaunty angle, rusts against the wall. At the other the shelves, once scrubbed for the pounding of butter, are covered by a history of dust.

Haste to the spinning house wherein ye will find the Ladies of ill repute.
There may they weave and spin in payment for their years of wickedness
and moral depravity.

Spinster: Unmarried woman. Note: Years of spinning ruined a woman's eyesight, thus rendering her unfit for marriage.

I write myself spinster because the laws of the land describe me thus.

How well I remember the sound of the churn. Phlumph . . . Phlumph rrr. Yet the spider, uncaring, continues to chart her days, her nights. The progressive explosion of technology means nothing to her.

Heads down, thigh deep in muck, men and women worked then for the bare few shillings at the end of the week. Now you either get the dole or throw a switch. No. That's urban lies. It's still toil, hard grieving toil, seven days a week, 365 days a year. Tractors, too, grow old and sluggish, and sometimes kill. Only the ranchers read books and throw switches.

Dear brother, hurrying to, hurrying fro, jotting, adding, subtracting, borrowing, buying, what category do you fall into?

Tonight I cook his favourite dinner — chops and potatoes and cauliflower cheese while he puts Jonathon to bed.

'He gets on well with you,' I offered, when he came down at last.

He sat down, untied the laces of his boots and cast his legs out in a V like a man rowing a boat. Seldom had I seen him so relaxed.

There was no inquisition, no castigation. I left him there and floated out into the night. There was still the remains of a smoky dusk as I crossed the stream by the rapids and on through

O'Reilly's stubble, the colour of burnt sugar in the eerie light. By skirting the wood heavy with its dark cracklings, dartings and breathings, I reached Lough Guenagh in about an hour. The light wind was shaking out the water and battalions of reeds marched into the edge till their tips were nearly submerged. Amongst them a solitary heron stood on a boulder. Beak down, wings tight, like a man with his hands in his pockets, he waited patiently for that moment when he would dive for his prey.

A shot rang out in the woods. Rooks lifted from the trees, hysterical, as from a long-drawn-out parliament, and the heron rose with deliberation and flew diagonally across the lake. In a few seconds all was quiet again. As if to accentuate this and close things for the night a white cushion of mist settled down on the lake.

But somewhere in the depths of that wood a man and a gun were lurking. Far away, the safety of kitchen, warmth of stove, strong reviving tea, Reynold's biscuits, even! I had gone out to leave him to his peaceful thoughts, now I regretted having wandered so far.

No moon, no stars. I could only hear the light snap as the small waves lapped at the edges of the shore. Everything had disappeared. I wasn't lost, naturally — I knew the way home as well as I knew the anatomy of my own body. But the dread of meeting another human creature lay heavy on me.

I began to blunder upwards towards the road. I wanted to get away from the woods ... the trees.

Once atop the field I could distinguish hazards, bushes, boulders and the like. Along here wound a thin road, called locally Cromwell's Road. Allegedly the latter had brought a battalion to stamp out a particularly recalcitrant local force. But the Irish were too clever by half. First of all they destroyed the battalion with their primitive weapons and escaped to the far shore in boats, leaving the English licking their wounds. Whether true or false, this tale, I was right glad of the road which would lead eventually to the main one between the two towns.

On the tarmac the going was easy, it cast a sheen in the leaden light. Like new sleeves sewn on to an old coat the village 'suburbs' fanned out both sides of the original street. The village, in my time, a cluster of four pubs which were also the local stores and sold everything from rubber boots to 'shop' bread, with the few dwellings in between, had now blossomed into another of these small midland towns. The garage at one end — although now a crazy sculpture of a steel awning and broken pumps because of lack of sales so near the border — and the chipper at the other to bid you hallo, goodbye. In between, the mini-supermarket, the butcher, the children's clothes shop, the four pubs, cast their orange glow on the pavements. The large tin-sheeted Co-op is a quarter mile outside the town, beyond which is the local authority housing estate and the 'lane' or 'avenue' to our farm.

As I passed the take-away, a cluster of teenagers stared solidly at me, mocked me when they thought I was out of earshot. I hurried on. I die a thousand deaths on these occasions. To them I was an old hag, far too old to feel anything, to me they were the judges of the universe.

Wary of the housing estate and similar taunts, I quickened my pace and wheeling past gratefully cut up home.

The kitchen was dark. What a lovely hour I spent, poking the range and dreaming. I was safe and sound, home at last. Well, that's how I thought about it anyway.

Jonathon is gone again, Reynold once more slotted into his self-imposed position. Boss of the ranch.

Yes, Deirdre and Gerald came to fetch their son. Reynold fussed with sherry and biscuits and chat was scattered round the sittingroom. Gerald and I discussed the ruin of the land by modern farming methods, chemicals and over-cultivation. Out of the corner of my eye I caught Reynold listening and I read his thoughts (greenpeace gobbledy-gook!). I spoke about my hens that were due to arrive the next day and how ridiculous it was that they had to come through Dublin, that you couldn't buy a free-range pullet in all of the county. But we also spoke of the tyranny of the old farm methods and the difference modern technology has made to the average small man. The three-roomed hovel, with the well a few hundred yards away, has been abandoned for the custom-built bungalow up on the ridge with running water and electric light. 'Only nuts, like artists and writers, would live in those hovels now.'

Again caught Reynold's eye but there was no hoped-for twinkle of approval.

The sherry warmed and swung the tongues, Deirdre, light from a weekend without her son, teased and cajoled her father till the latter — in spite of my presence — was forced to allow undisciplined smiles to weave across his cheeks. He alternatively sniffed and bit his short moustache, bouncing Jonathon on his knee, holding the child's two shoulders like an accordion.

'Reynold has been marvellous with Jonathon,' I said. But when they left Gerald thanked me and said if ever I was in Dublin they had a spare room.

'Goodbye, old chap,' Reynold called as the child was bundled into the car and it buzzed off scattering pebbles in all directions. But, as soon as they were out of sight, he turned on his heel, exchanging no words, and went off about his business.

I finished the henhouse in the nick of time. It has the illusion of being a fine shed. At least there are angles and matching squares — the perches neatly dove-tailed into the wooden cross-sticks at either end, nesting boxes warmly lining the party wall. And they've arrived. My hens. Rhode Island reds. A dozen glossy pullets with auburn feathers. They settled in without questioning the reason. If promises can be believed they should lay in about three weeks.

In the afternoon I let them out. Shooed into the yard they pecked about like dowagers on a cruise. I have a revulsion against battery chickens, the yellow smell, the cheeping that rings all day. And when they're done laying they're shipped alive to England to be sold as boilers for the poor. Looking at them I felt immensely proud, as if I'd achieved something way beyond my dreams.

A mere dozen hens and a friendly chat with Arthur. It doesn't take much to raise my spirits!

Shortly after this I was blessed with a few days' peace. Reynold went off to Dublin for the best part of a week.

I took it easy. The weather was warm and sunny. I began breaking soil in the old garden, surprised to find how loose the earth was still. I worried about the fox, and decided that I must dig down some netting wire round my chicken coop.

The thought of a jaunt to town had put Reynold in a good mood. He even acknowledged my worth by asking me to change the bullocks from the hill field to the one across the avenue.

A torture of a job. They cast up their backsides, tricking and farting as dogless and friendless I zig-zagged hither and thither, climbing and re-climbing the barbed wire fence. Finally the bastards got the message and trickled into their new quarters and immediately started to graze like children loosed at a tea party.

The netting wire was difficult to dig into the ground. There was too much rubble round the shed. Eventually I gave in and retired to make my supper.

I turned on Radio Three and was settling in to a relaxed evening when an infernal cackle in the yard made me fly out in terror. Only a week and my chickens were being.... Inside the hen house stood Cathy, the hens screeching, feathers choking the atmosphere.

'What the fuck do you think you're at?'

She didn't move, just stood scuffing the sawdust floor with the toe of her shoe.

'Cathy!'

'Come on. I'm not going to hit you.' Oh, the control, the calm voice of logic.

Single file, she leading, we entered the kitchen. She went straight over to the window and stared out.

She smoothed her cotton skirt — she was wearing a T-shirt through which her nipples poked like berries — and the skirt, a dirty yellow, had little maps of mud-stains running down the back. Her runners were broken at the sides.

'You could do with a new pair of shoes,' I said as I put out the tea things, slicing up bread I had recently baked.

She drifted to the table, sat down and contemplated the bread as though she would have preferred sliced pan.

'And by the way, I'm not doling out charity chickens to you or anyone else for that matter. You've never seen me angry but if I get angry with you you'll never come up here again. So don't push your luck.'

Her wide nostrils flared as she piled butter and jam on to the bread, allowing crumbs to cluster each side of her mouth, and took gulps of tea, sloshing down the cup so that it spilled on to the tablecloth.

'What size shoes do you take?'

'Fours.'

I felt my limbs loosening, like a cat withdrawing its claws.

Got up and walked over to her. 'You're a real ice maiden tonight, Cathy.'

I pulled a chair up beside hers. She looked away. 'Come on.'

'I didn't mean to ...' the phrase blurted out, settled in the air as though it had a life of its own.

'Oh, for heaven's sake, I don't blame you.'

'Don't you?' The nipples moved, her shoulders nudged forward. If she had wept I would have hugged her then, but she did not.

I got up, stacked the dishes, wiped away the debris, shook out the cloth, folded it into four and poked it into the dresser drawer.

'Go,' I said. 'Go home. I'll see you tomorrow.' I kept my back to her.

It was already dark though the night was mild and sticky. I

opened the door and wandered out, leaving her alone. I paused at the window. Like the sea receding over polluted rocks her face seemed unnaturally exposed. Although I stared and stared I saw neither contrition nor anger in her expression, just nothing.

But when I came back in she jumped up, looking frightened again, and darted past me without a word. I saw her pass the window, the flash of her T-shirt like a blank page waiting to be filled.

I ran out, called, 'Goodbye, Cathy,' into the funnel of darkness.

Ferociously lonely, I snapped shut the outer door, closed out the night, the leaf-rustling, the cattle lamenting, the imagined steps of the half-demented young/old Cathy, her own front door opening, closing, the vinegar of half-digested beer, the squabbling of children, the mother, distraught, Jim, the 'bad blood' circling and circling his body, standing aside, a prisoner in his own inheritance.

Swivelled the knobs of the radio, nothing only country and western from pirate stations, talk on the proposed hospice for dying children, an angry wailing from a pop singer, the crackling and whistling of foreign stations. Knocked off the switch, dead, uneasy silence.

Another day without Reynold. I did what I'd been postponing doing since I arrived. Visited father's room.

There was a queer stacked look about the place as though someone had come in in a hurry after the funeral and tidied everything furtively. The bed was pushed to a corner — the large double bed in which he and mother, and then he alone, had slept all his years here. A few books in piles, not in a shelf. Two chairs — the one upside down on the other. The dressing table with the mirror, again pushed against the wall — once it had stood well out into the room. I opened the clothes cupboard.

His suits hung in a row from the cross-rail, the jackets dapper on their hangers, the trousers neat as knives folded underneath.

I laid them out on the bed, going through the pockets one by one. I thought they were all empty and was surprised to find a letter in one of the inner pockets. It was typed — no doubt some business correspondence that the over-zealous tidier hadn't noticed.

In the chest of drawers, little sachets of white handkerchiefs, balls of socks, vests, Y-fronts, all neatly folded as though they'd just come from the shop, lay in rows.

In the lower one, his shirts, again folded. White ones, striped ones and two or three in policeman blue cotton.

My grandfather had been a fervent gambler. From him, obviously, father had inherited his love of the Turf. He followed the doctrine of money gained easily being the money most to be praised. He gambled on horses, cards, and finally the stock-exchange.

So my father, following in his footsteps, must, however, have been reasonably astute. I could picture him now, in one of these dapper suits, a white mac slung easily over his shoulder, calculating odds at the foot of one of the course bookies. I could see him, racecard to his lips, turning to look at the list of jockeys, turning back to the bookmaker and placing a tenner or a fiver on the chosen one. Ten pounds win African Dancer, and the bookies striking the odds down from fours to threes.

Although he was in his eighties, these were not the clothes of an old man expecting to die soon, nor of a man who drank to excess and smoked heavily. They appeared to belong to a man with a zest for living, someone who should have had a mistress or girl-friend tucked away in the city, only too pleased to accompany him to Leopardstown, Naas or the Curragh, who would dine later the same evening in a not too ostentatious restaurant. But there was no word of any flat or hide-out which he might have used.

I was somewhat discomposed by these relics. It was as though a complete stranger was sitting there on the bed, watching me with a faint smile. And yet . . . it was the sad remains of a life — if not wasted — of very little account. Early retirement from the civil service and living, presumably, on the gains of his father, he shuttle-cocked between this place and the city, one week telescoped into the next, one year no different from the last until that day a bare six weeks ago when, turning the ignition in his car, he had had a massive heart attack. Mrs Mulvaney had found him slumped over the steering-wheel later that same afternoon.

If I had cared for him, I could have wept. How lonely this house is when it is empty. No wonder he spent so much time away and let the place run to seed. Would I do the same if my enemy brother weren't here? Would I drink myself into a dish-cloth, give up washing, looking in the mirror, eating? Or would I steal gradually back into my old ways, picking up alcoholic psychopaths who would drag me into the old sexual morass? Or would I soldier on, painting, scrubbing, cooking, feeding my hens and planting herbs?

I put everything back into its place. Another day, another time to decide what to do with these remains. The suits were too small for Reynold; the only person I could think of was Gerald, Dierdre's husband. But perhaps he wouldn't like to wear a dead man's clothes.

Finally I went over to the mirror, wiping it with my sleeve. Up until now I had smugly believed that I could mould myself into the landscape as though I weren't there, or rather as though I were invisible, but now seeing the ravages that time had played with my face I was staggered. This is what Reynold sees every day. This ragged countenance, this scar, that wild hair with wedges of grey straying in and out of its original black. A whole wasted life seemed to stare back through those eyes. But no! I wanted to shout again: there are strong years ahead. I turned to face the room again, and again I fancied my father sitting there and laughing at me. You bastard. Because of you I was banished, self-exiled, re-rooted in a country that could never be mine. But I'm back and single-handed will persist in my quest, my *peau de chagrin*.

I wandered over to the window, looked at the spot on which I had stood the last time we saw each other.

'You're going away to win the war?' The sarcasm of the drawn back lips, the sniff, the exposed lower teeth.

'I'm going.'

The bag on the back of my bicycle, my hands on the handle-bars, we stood a yard from each other. He expected me to embrace him. I did not. He did not step towards me. Constance had gone on ahead to hold the bus. It was ten minutes to ten. A windy October morning. The leaves still clung to the trees, wild with autumnal colour. I bumped down the avenue. The rain which threatened held off. I was sixteen and a half years old, heavy-haired, narrow-bodied, plain-faced, neat-footed. Thus we parted. He did not watch me go. I did not look back.

I stayed at the window then, older than he was when we had parted those long years ago, and I pictured how an onlooker might look up and see this crazy face at the window. Indeed I remembered a remark of Deirdre's which I'd forgotten to record earlier: 'Why don't you shut her up like Mrs Rochester, in the attic?' A fine pair of fish-wives, she and her father! To accompany this generous thought of mine there was a blinding flash followed at once by a thunder-clap that seemed to knock the house sideways. The sky lit up with electric forks followed by crash upon crash.

When the rain started, it pelted down in vertical rods, tearing into the gulleys, leaping off the cobblestones. My hens, who had been pecking aimlessly, scattered, their bodies low from the weight of water crashing on them.

As suddenly it stopped and the thunder rolled away, the blanket of cloud cleared and a watery sun lit up the devastation, puddles, dripping trees, leaking drainpipes, and the smell of lush and loam wafted up through the open window. The God-forsaken dump had at least been washed clean.

Would my cat-black soul be similarly cleansed, I wondered, as I took one last look at this room — their room — and like a bar across my chest I was reminded of my mother, of whom I thought as infrequently as possible, and the look of resigned boredom that crept over her features every time I entered the room. How that woman hated me. And how when at last she gave in to the cancer that had spread all over her, her death was tidied away along with the syringes, the bottles, the powders, the methylated spirit for the bedsores, the smells. And how this room, yes, this room, had been made airtight with sticking paper and sprayed with formaldehyde. For a few nights he had slept downstairs and when the disinfection was done, moved back. And this was his bedroom until he died.

With difficulty I extricated myself from my stance. Like the recent flood, my memories had begun to drown what common sense was left in me.

And that very evening when a modicum of calm had invested itself in the sky and the sun shone as though it meant it, I went looking for Cathy.

I was afraid. My heart was doing queer things as though the cells in my bloodstream were off balance and colliding with each other in crazy trafficking. I was afraid she might not be in her usual hideout, that my over-careful dealings with her the previous day had been too transparent. But she was there, drowned out of all recognition, hair and clothes plastered on her.

'Why didn't you come up to the house? You knew "Mister" was away.'

'I were afraid.' *She* was afraid?

'Come on then now.'

She came eagerly, running before me, the wet garments rattling like mail, when in the house, left puddles on the floor.

As I dried her hair I felt the hunger in her. That she had deliberately refused to shelter, waited for the rain to enter every crevice of her body, and then again stood in the very spot where we nearly always meet, showed the pain of her need. And I hungered then to know, 'Does she love me, does she really love me?'

My jeans were too long for her and she laughed as she slopped around barefoot, muddying the ends of them.

'At least you could roll them up.' For the first time, it seemed, mutual amusement took us over. She looked almost attractive in my bulky Aran sweater, her hair standing up in damp corkscrew curls. I put her miserable shoes on the Rayburn to dry, having filled them with balls of newspaper. Her mucky clothes I threw into the sink.

The radio blared out pop music. Chords chased one on top of another, a cracked voice wailed. Cathy jumped on the table and began to dance.

Energy collected in a ball inside me. I rang for the village taxi and we went to town. We ate cheesecake and lemon meringue pie and drank cups of real coffee. We saw a film that she'd always wanted to see — *Rocky*. We ate right through the film, chocolates, sweets and icecream. Satiated with emotion and sugar we emerged into a starry night. The town, having disgorged all its teenagers on the pavements, vibrated with their catcalls.

'I'd like to be rich,' Cathy said, as we zig-zagged through them.

'What's the first thing you'd do with your money?'

'I'd take us far away.'

I held a space in time, parting the air with my hands, like a row of books pressing against two bookends.

'Where would we go?'

'To Asia.'

I glimpsed my ragged face in a shop window, glanced at Cathy. Her face was parted and open, like I'd never seen it before.

Let me die first . . . or let us both die together. My oft repeated prayer as a child when thinking of my sister. My whole woeful life was with me in that second as I remembered that prayer.

We walked cautiously to the street where the two town taxis might be found, the ferocious pain of not touching her twisting my gut beneath my ribs as though I'd been kicked in the solar plexus.

Nor did I hug her in the taxi although she huddled near me, the peculiar wet-earth smell of her a torment.

She hummed a little and then fell into silence, remembering the battle ahead of her.

'You could stay with me.' The last tongues of light from the street lamps had long been swallowed up behind us and savouring the noise of the engine on the dark empty road I knew that I must stop this obsession before it got altogether beyond my control.

Was I freed then of my need for her? Even temporarily?

During the last few miles of the journey I tried to bring her family alive by questioning her. Though even as I questioned I felt no interest in her life beyond the periphery of my vision. Out of my sight she might not have existed. If I thought about her mother at all it was of a gaunt overworked overweight matron in a blue dress with varicose veins and the ladder of children streeling along behind.

Suddenly she said, 'Me da's even worse in the mornings'.

And it was then I caught a glimpse of a middle-sized man with skin like that of a swede turnip, hair dull as winter grass, and the shock of anger never far from his expression.

'What would happen if I went in and explained? You could lay all the blame on me.'

'Oh no.' Horror curdled her speech. The taxi had slowed down; we were entering the housing estate.

'No, drive on. Up there, to the left,' I called out and we cut up the avenue and were dumped in the darkness of the yard.

As the house sprang into life I led her up the stairs to my sister's room where Jonathon had recently slept. She undressed quickly and jumped into bed. I brushed her brow with my lips.

Damn it! I came here to retire from such, to work, drill, plough, mend fences, spray potatoes, all those tasks I did as a girl, knew well how to do. What I learnt over there — how to restore old furniture, decorate, and renew rooms — was only one extension of what I learnt here as a child. What had I got myself into? How many more times was this going to happen to me?

When eventually I slept I dreamt of the anointing of my own dead body. Freud, no doubt, would have had a field day on this.

It was afternoon when the scrunching on the gravel whipped reality back on me. He blustered in in a flurry of parcels, papers, put them down, went out for more. Backing and parking the neat way he liked it. The engine roared.

'My exhaust box is hanging off.' Reynold beamed round the room like a lighthouse.

'I should maybe contact the county council. She if they will share the price of filling the potholes.'

'You do that, old girl.'

He was like a child who couldn't stop chuckling. I wondered was he feverish.

'There's a fridge in the car.'

'Did you buy one?'

'I ripped it out of my flat.'

So he still kept his flat. Here was a rose-tinted piece of news.

He went off upstairs 'to change into something comfortable.'

A wrapped bottle stood among the parcels. Whiskey.

I tidied away the purchases. Some exciting new tools had to be stacked above eye-level.

Never a musical man, my brother, he descended the stairs with a hum like a cat's purr on his lips.

'Can I bring in the fridge?'

'Sure.' As we awkwardly unloaded it he asked me where I would like it put.

'You're looking well. Any news?'

'There was a thunderstorm.'

'Really? Nothing like that in Dublin.'

'Must have been local.'

Strips of small talk were being bandied round the room while he emptied out his pockets on the table. Money, cigarettes, pieces of paper.

'These are your favourite brand, I think.' He tendered two packets of twenty cigarettes.

'Very kind of you.'

'How about a little snifter each? I'm sure you've had a busy day.'

He took two glasses from the dresser and with the dish towel rubbed them carefully, holding them up against the light after doing so. With a flourish he peeled the silver wrapper from round the cork of the whiskey bottle.

'Do you take water?'

The pale gold liquid swam from side to side as he held it up.

'Thanks.'

He knocked his back neat and poured himself another.

'You accomplished some business happily, I gather.' No longer able to contain my curiosity, which was tinged with dread, the whiskey loosened my tongue.

'What, what?' he pretended to be busy checking off a list.

'It's something to do with me?' The air had suddenly become oppressive. I got up and opened a window — a moist southerly wind was gathering the leaves of the beech tree into a whispering mass.

'I ... er, well ...'

'You're sketching in the shading first. Give it to me now, Reynold.'

'I saw Forbes.'

'Yes?'

'Well, father had another ten thousand in shares which have come to light.'

'How did he do it? Perhaps it was just as well he didn't farm the place. He might have spend it all on hare-brained schemes.'

'Well, he left them to you after Constance disappeared.'

'Why on earth...?'

'So you could ... so you'd be able...'

The lethargy following a lost battle. I rose wearily.

'You could just about buy yourself an acre or two...'

'No, Reynold. It doesn't matter...' Each word was now an ache in my temples.

'But there's no hurry. Stay till spring.'

'Excuse me.' I went out into the yard, the tiny muscles of my eyes expanding and contracting. I would never weep in front of Reynold no more than Cathy would weep in front of me.

It's not his fault. No, it's not his fault. Perhaps I have no centre, no impetus. The muscles in my calves ached as though I had cycled a huge distance. I crouched by the broken wall. More thunder rolled. Then came the feathery touch of rain on my bare arm, warm at first, gradually cooling.

It was a crazy wound. It wouldn't heal. Perhaps a cancer would grow there instead, some day, and switch me off.

Arthur had become a regular Sunday visitor. Reynold had taken up golf. A new club had opened up in the nearest large town.

Arthur talked about 'guilty consciences'.

'To think that I really have got the money Constance should have had is hard to take. Especially since the father didn't believe that she was murdered.'

'Revenge is a terrible thing.'

I looked sideways at him. He was plucking snowberries and bursting them between finger and thumb. He had seen much of it over the last fifteen years, I knew, but would never talk of it. Silence only is safe.

'Take no notice of your brother. Plough the money into the farm.'

Plough is right. I laughed to lighten the conversation. Only too easily does the negative possess me and Reynold's loop-hole, as I had begun to call it, seemed the negation of my life.

Revenge!

In a flash I imagined the small house she and her husband lived in. Tastefully furnished like herself — always tastefully dressed — and both of them in bed upstairs. I imagined the balaclavaed faces, eyes flashing, the spray of petrol, the immediate conflagration, the heat, the smoke, the sky lit up, the noise of falling masonry.

Revenge!

And the screams!

Father calling up the solicitor and adding a codicil to his will. To my daughter, Dilligence Strong . . .

'By the way,' I began. We were approaching the river, intending to cross by the rapids as a short cut into McDonagh's farm to make a deal over the bonhams. 'You remember her charm. Perhaps you liked her better than . . .' I stopped.

He took my arm.

'You were the more intriguing . . . very shy at first . . . Both of you were . . . how shall I put it . . .'

'A bit over the top?'

'Perhaps wild.' My body began to unfreeze, my face shorten.

'A right pair, in fact.' But even speaking about her made the old jealousy return. As if to reassure me he reiterated:

'You were just as attractive as her. Different. You were a great one for making up the stories. Always had something in your head.' I laughed.

'That's what Reynold says. I'm a compulsive liar, he thinks.'

'You are still attractive.' I didn't want this although my spine tingled. I even felt secretly amused, elated almost. Abruptly, however, I changed the subject.

I began to imagine him in bed. The very clean underwear, his milky smell. Was he too nice? I suddenly realised I had never been in bed with a 'nice' man. It would be an interesting experience. Nice. Nicely. What horrible words. No, it was unfair to dismiss him as merely 'nice'. I remembered the sloes and I knew he could take me if he wanted to.

I asked him about the Magees and he told me or, rather, implied that Mr Magee could be dangerous in drink but that the mother was a fine woman — determined to bring up the kids properly (I wondered how Cathy fitted into this category) — but was hard put to make ends meet. She went out cleaning to augment the few bob on the dole. I asked him why she didn't throw him out. My easy urban solution to all ills. He ended up by saying: 'I wouldn't have anything to do with that crowd'.

No, 'nice' is the wrong word. Just because he is sympathetic towards me I call him 'nice'. How easily I become all the things I despise most. Self-deprecating, craving crumbs of affection. He treats me with warmth because he actually likes me! No fool, Arthur. Always circumspect. In face of his kind of rural intelligence all those clichés about men and power and guns and penises, all those dismissive sentences mouthed when people are holed up in some urban pub, seemed mighty unsubtle.

When he left that day he left me in an expectant state. I went down the violet flank of the wood. The trees shift with long sighs and I always fear a shot or a dark shape that might turn out to be a stranger. But I had to wander to clear my mind. The heron was at his usual perch, sentinel of the lake, the crows silent in the trees. Gulls dipped and feinted above the water. Soon they too would disappear when the dark became absolute. A fish jumped, a large perch or a small pike. There was a scatter of birds and a gull's long cry. When the necklace of ripples left by the fish had subsided the lake resumed its black crepuscular sheen. The sky was overcast. Since the storm the temperature had dropped, a touch of winter. Many of the crops had been laid. The pleasant afternoon with Arthur was soon forgotten when darkness fell. Dully I watched the reeds disappearing into the night, the lake going dim. I couldn't shake off the memory of Reynold's news and his continued hostility.

Sometimes on a night like this the earth seems to give a jerk and all the individual night calls communicate themselves to each other. As I stood then a sudden cacophony of sound came from all sides. The braying of a donkey, the lowing of a cow, the call of a mallard or water hen till again silence.

I seem to be drawn to this inhospitable place late at night. Once more I faced the choice of two evils — the return through the village or the mud and slush of the journey through the forest. How was it that I never bring a torch on these occasions?

Unable to face the village I struggled home through ruts, sliding and slipping and occasionally catching my hair in a branch. My thoughts ran on pretty hopeless lines. I knew I must keep on fighting my patch but now I seemed to have got myself totally involved with Cathy. Was she becoming too dependent on me — Rabbit bones. Was it mutual? But, I argued, I can't bear to talk to her for more than five minutes yet I wanted her with me. When she wasn't there I went searching for her. My doppelganger, lying, scheming, sly little alter-ego.

Perhaps it was as well she wasn't there on that recondite night.

After this ferocious journey I sat long by the Rayburn, glad to be out of the dark yet angry at the realisation that there was maybe no solution to my many problems.

Next morning I was in a fever. I tried to drag myself out of bed but the room spun like a postcard stand. Pain, pain everywhere. A giant pliers grappled my skull. My hips, my back, my shoulders ached. Sleep came in sporadic balls of oblivion, dream and nightmare. My throat seared as though it had been gouged with a scalpel. All day I made little trips to the bathroom. Around four (I think) Reynold poked his head in, stood awkwardly, offered to send for the doctor, which I refused. A little later he brought me tea. It tasted as though it had been stirred with wet string. Tried to get it down to please him but it cooled quickly and I left it.

When he came again, I don't know how many hours later, he removed the half-full cup.

'Sorry.' My voice half an octave lower than usual.

'No need to get up. No need at all.' He was relieved to have me out of the way, the place to himself at last.

Visions of early days of great-uncles and aunts, my mother withdrawn as a nun, my father's only sister, Aunty Mel, who had a mole on the left side of her chin from which grew a corkscrew of hair. It was she who lent over me and said, 'You deliberately tore up the photograph'. What photograph?

It was Mick O'Shea who came next. I had shared bed and board with him in London for a while. He was thumping out discordant sounds on a guitar and I said, 'I didn't know you could play that'. I longed for him to be quiet.

He leant over me, pulled my arm. I woke up and saw Reynold again. This time he'd concocted some thin soup from a packet.

'Is it raining?' I asked. He nodded while he held me up. It also tasted woolly and every swallow was cut by the razor nestling at the back of my throat.

'You've been muttering.' I attempted a laugh.

'They all came'. Shapes and forms to count, prophesy not doom, exactly, but to tell you again and again that you're digging your own grave. But did they? I mean make better lives for themselves?

'I ought to have got the doctor.'

He placed his palm on my forehead. He had never done that before. As a child he had placed pillows over my head and ever since I've had a terror of being buried alive.

His hand on my forehead made me unspeakably content.

Then I was thrown back into the net of nightmare.

'Aunt Mel had one leg. Father called her a great old warhorse.'

He retrieved his hand. I think he must have left the room, because I said, 'Water.' Nothing happened.

I once opened a cupboard and there was a large deal leg standing there as if brooding for companionship.

'Why didn't Aunt Mel wear the false leg, do you know?'

That was a clear sensible question and I heard myself ask it aloud. 'Why didn't she?' When Gertrude Stein was dying she asked Alice B. Toklas, What is the answer? When Toklas didn't say anything, Stein then asked, What is the question?

'But there was no information and so we continued.'

'You're still feverish.'

There he was again. Should I ask him for water? I woke widely. 'Am I being morbid?'

'You're doing a lot of chattering.' He almost laughed.

I kicked at the bedclothes. They were wet and heavy like a dog lying on me. I could feel the sweat at the rim of my hair line.

'I'm better. I know I'm on the mend.'

'Good, good.'

'How long have I been ill?'

'Three days.'

'No? Honestly?'

This time I heaved myself up.

'It's daylight,' I exclaimed.

I was emaciated from my illness. Each day seemed greyer than the last. When eventually my bones stopped aching I attempted a walk.

She was there.

'I thought you were never coming.'

I imagined her frozen in one position for days like the little Match Girl.

'I'm sorry. I had a fever.'

She looked very serious. Old. How old is she, how young am I? We drifted through the strip of chestnut trees. Her feet dragged more than mine. She was identifying with my illness, perhaps jealous of it.

'My brother was never a child.'

'How so?' Her voice, glum.

'He never knew the mischief of innocence.'

'Will you die before him?'

'I don't know.'

We walked a few yards in silence.

'I'm going to die.'

'You are not.'

'Oh yes, Dilly. I am.' She started running.

'Cathy,' I called. 'Stop.'

She wouldn't though, would she?

Like a puddle drying up in the sun what little energy I had deserted me. I sat down on a greasy stump.

Should I leave here and take her with me? My money would last a couple of years. Then maybe I could persuade her to learn something, to be self-supporting. But that small amount of speculation wearied me. I had tried to propitiate Reynold and failed. The fact that my pullets had started laying had given me the greatest pleasure but that had ended with my illness. OK, I had succeeded in organising fresh eggs by courtesy of twelve young hens. Hats off to hens and me lying as sick as a dog unable to move for over a week. What sort of victory was that?

'Go home then, Cathy, go home.'

For three days I kicked about doing nothing. No sign of her although I stumbled up the hill every day. Slow, slow convalescence! What lethargy. It reminded me of a man called McPhillips. Roger. From Armagh. He induced this kind of lethargy in me. Younger than I and when he went to town puffed out like a pigeon I had to tie up my nerve ends with gins and tonics. If you have a shop at the back end of Brixton that's bound to be the middle of a story. No neat conclusions — pleasant beginnings.

Reynold complains about the lack of home-made bread but treats me like a valuable Spode teapot. He has a way with sick people but he tends to think I'm shamming (I think) after all these days. A little less patient when he found there was no bread. And yet I assured him I had baked my usual quantity. (Which I had.)

My walks became manic. Every footstep tired me but I searched and searched. Perhaps her father had shut her in again. If only that were the reason. Or if that were the only reason.

Ho, blessed illness when I lived four whole days outside my reason.

Such a simple thing as allowing my feet to get wet on a cold night used as a catalyst to Reynold's news, the complexities of my relationships temporarily shelved.

But now, back in my normal paranoiac state, I have to fend off my demons once again.

I decided to bake more bread.

As I searched for Cathy I kept saying, *But there was no information and so we continued*.

Reynold was already in bed, presumably asleep, a couple of nights later. I was half crazed with worry. Perhaps her statement: I am going to die, was really serious? But no, I refused to believe it.

As usual the bread had disappeared so I took down the flour and was about to fill the bowl when I heard something. A noise like a creature in pain — a kind of wild groan.

I stood quite still, watching. Watching the door.

Then it came again, a terrible roar and with this the door burst open. It was Mr Magee. Drunk, staggering, waving a shotgun.

'Where is she, you bitch you? I know she's fucking here. You and your evil ways. You's'll answer for this.'

I was terrified. I knew if I made a false move he could kill me. Death! There was death in his face — his eyes wild, his skin taut and stippled with broken veins. His clothes were torn, muddy — I could smell him although he was still a few feet away.

I tried to speak, to cry out 'No', but the saliva had dried up in my mouth.

I began to back away. Slowly.

Slowly he advanced.

'Please,' I managed at last, my voice a low growl. 'She's not here.'

I was hurled across the room, a fierce pain rode up my shoulder where I had hit the table. He was leaning over me, breathing into my face, muttering, cursing, 'Thems that should have owned the land in the first place should have it now.' Protestant acres, Protestant cows, Protestant fences. I backed away further, my hands protecting my face.

Suddenly he wheeled away, turned and went running up the stairs.

I screamed then. I was terrified that Reynold would hear him or even that if he found my brother in bed he'd kill him. I screamed again and he came back down and left the house. But not without a final insinuation that somehow or other I wielded some power over his daughter and that we were evil people and should be run out of the county.

He was gone.

It's impossible to describe my feelings of reprieve. My bones were like rubber. All I know is I couldn't rise. What I don't know is how long I sat in the chair. The interval of time between his leaving and Reynold's appearing might have been a day and a half but was only about half an hour.

'I told her, I told her to go,' I kept muttering to myself, when Reynold in dressing gown and slippers was standing in the inner doorway.

'Very late up. Did I hear something? I was woken up by something and couldn't get back to sleep.'

Used, by now, to my catatonic appearance, he simply raised his nostrils, saying do I smell tea?

Reynold doesn't stink of failure like Mr Magee.

Where is Cathy?

The bread?

Reynold put water in the kettle.

Reynold talked.

'I've made a deal over the hill field. Set it for the winter. The bullocks will do below. Anyway come in for the winter.'

I couldn't follow the logic.

We needed the field for winter grazing. I tried to lift my head from the palm of my hand.

'Where?' was all I managed.

'Dilly, are you asleep? Have you had a relapse?'

'No, no. The shed needs re-roofing.' Is that what I meant?

'Begley's son is coming up to do it tomorrow.'

'Is that the one at Agricultural College?' Without turning my head which was so heavy I just swivelled my eyes at him.

'Yes. We'll fix it together.'

Begley's son is coming to fix the shed. We'll fix it together. Brother on the roof. This was funny. I felt a spiral of laughter surging up through my whole body. I ran out, shaking convulsively. How my legs held me up I do not know. All I remember is that once out of earshot I allowed the hysteria to run its course.

When I came to, I was leaning against a tree, wet through with sobs and pee and sweat.

Now I must find her. God knows what he'd do to her if he found her first.

There was one place I hadn't looked, an old unused shed at the far end of our river field. Long before our time it had been a boathouse. There was also the old glue mill about a mile up the river. But everyone said it was haunted so I doubted she'd dare to hide there.

I found myself running, scraping through briar and nettle — my arm throbbed but I ignored it.

The shed was empty except for some rusty junk. I circled back, calling hopelessly.

Perhaps she had got away. Got right away.

Reynold was still up, warming his pyjama-clad shins by the Rayburn.

'Are you sure you're all right?' It was difficult not to blurt out the whole happening, the horror, the obscenity of Mr Magee. But I'd be the one to suffer. I wished he'd go back to bed. Since Reynold had played his trump card he had become positively friendly. I would have given anything for him to stay like that.

At last he got up and went.

Just as I was about to rake the range and fill it for the night, she came. A small scraping at the door like a twig loosed from its branch. I froze. Supposing it were him back, more crazed than ever? This time he'd do for me. In his bones he sheltered generations of bitterness. Others around might hold that we were decent folk, but not Mr Magee. For the likes of him there's only black and white, narrow, bitter, no room for tolerance.

I waited, stiff, breathless for other sounds till it came again. That weak scraping. 'Is it you?'

'Aye.'

Her face was all dirty, the skin the colour of a soiled bandage, her clothes dung-marked.

'My God! You're in a state.' But there was no time for explosions of emotion or horror. She had to be fed. Plans had to be formed. As she ate, her shoulders moved independently like squirrels. She held the cup in both hands, her neat nails, black-half-mooned at the tips, lifted and fell as though she were playing the tin whistle. She had lost weight and her broad face looked absurd with its tousled hair stuck on top of the string-like body.

She had found a ruin over a mile and a half beyond McDonagh's land. There in the cow shit and broken timber she had sheltered, coming up here for bits of food when Reynold and I were in bed.

'Did he come here?' Her voice parched with apprehension.

'He did.'

'Did he have a . . .'

I wanted to reassure her that he wouldn't harm her, that her only chance was to go home when he was in bed. But how could I send her into that web of danger? Even if he slept off his drunkenness, in the morning he'd crawl out, dry-mouthed, double-visioned, hoarse with excuses tempered with abuse. For a short while I had experienced such a man, who, had I not left him, would have wrung me out like an old sock. He had wormed his way into my affections, a base-less Irishman, handsome as a pirate, would remove money from the till as though it were his priestly due and treat me to all kinds of gaieties. For a while we swashbuckled around the town like Bonnie and Clyde until just too much drink had been downed, too much laughter laughed, and then the degradation would start, the abuse, the cursing, the beating, the kicking. No, no, there must be some other solution for Cathy. Such a man as Cathy's father, when blinded by his own failure, will stop at nothing.

Plans skirled round my head like gulls on the lake.

Never did I feel so friendless. Not a sinner did I know in the country on whom I could rely to look after her. To send her to England might be too big a step for her to handle. Besides, she is imbued with hatred of the oppressor, this her father had instilled in her. Her dependence on me is only a step towards the destruction of my kind. My dependence on her is of another order. My duty now is to free her from all softness.

'Have you any relations in the North?'

'My cousin Fan.'

'Where?'

She mentioned a town in Tyrone.

'And what's your auntie like?'

'All right.'

'Have you stayed there ever?'

'When I was little.'

It emerged that she and the three younger ones had gone there with her mother. Her mother had planned to run away for ever. But the house was too small and they had returned to face the music.

'If you went there now would she send you back?'

How could Cathy answer this? But it seemed the merest thread of hope. It had to be tried.

I explained that I'd give her money and put some aside for her keep. She said she'd try to get work. She'd go to night-school to learn a skill of some kind.

When fed and warm and equipped with a blanket, she slipped out into the night.

As she raced beyond the periphery of the dim light cast by the kitchen window, I could imagine her ducking and feinting amongst the bushes that crawled half-way down our field and crossing the sturdy barbed wire and thorn fence into his big ten-acre meadow and beyond, over another fence into the short wet expanse she had to negotiate before she reached the ruined cabin.

How must I admit that the bit of my life that she took then was only another microcosm, a shambles of events that have gone to make up the whole? Reynold, for all his fumbling moralising and easy summarizing, is not far off in his assessment of my character. All my life I've gone blind into cul-de-sacs.

Cathy, Arthur, Reynold, so many lines of doubt lead from me to these people. I am an old woman in a hurry but I have a long way to go.

I looked at the clock. It had turned 3 a.m. I felt no desire to sleep but knew I must make an effort, otherwise I'd never face the morning. As I climbed the stairs I felt something in my pocket. A letter. What letter could this be?

As I got into bed I opened it.

It was the letter I'd taken from my father's pocket and had

forgotten all about.

I was only vaguely curious (it started off Dear Jim) till I turned it over and my heart nearly stopped beating.

It was from Constance.

The first page was taken up with a long description of a race-meeting in the North. And how she had gone home fifty pounds the richer. But the second page was more personal. She wondered had the 'demon' Reynold showed his face recently and that she had a desperate work-load at the moment and wouldn't be able to get down for a few weeks.

I turned it back to page one to look at the date. There wasn't one.

I felt a moment of profound sadness. Sadness for both of them. She who would die (no doubt her last letter to her father) probably quite soon afterwards and he also dead now. Never would I make my peace with either of them.

But I couldn't help smiling at her sly reference to Reynold. If she'd mentioned me, however, she might have said something worse. I was glad not to know how she thought of me. That is if she ever thought of me at all. I put the envelope under my pillow and fell into a deep sleep.

Reynold seldom goes for walks. But the following night he wasn't in for his supper. I'd managed to sneak off and feed Cathy and I was trying to carry on as if there was nothing amiss.

A whole day had passed and still I had made no decision about her.

Any minute her father might show up, a drunken madman. I paced the floor. I worried now about Reynold. Where the hell was he? Mr Magee would no doubt think that he was in on the act — as he imagined — of kidnapping his daughter. I sat down stiffly, listening for any unusual sound.

Perhaps Reynold was in the house. Sick? I ran to the foot of the stairs and shouted. I went into the yard to see was there a light on in his room. No sign of that.

I tried to relax, turned on the radio. I had to switch it off immediately because it interfered with my concentration.

'You called?'

'Where were you?'

'How do you mean where was I?'

'Just wondered.'

'Dilly, your behaviour over the last couple of days has been extremely odd. You're hiding something.'

'And,' when I didn't reply, 'For your information I was in the attic.'

'The attic?'

If it were he asking me what I was doing I'd have to tell him. But I, so programmed, didn't dare ask.

He had a mouldy-looking book under his arm.

'And do you know what this is?'

'Some sort of notebook.'

'It's a diary. And do you know to whom this diary belonged?'

'You, I suppose.' What next?

'Well, it's not mine.'

'It belonged to Constance?'

'Exactly.'

Fortuitous conundrum. Obviously he had unearthed something with an evil slant on me. His eyes were narrowed, and he had a smile that wasn't humorous. He looked like one who makes a final bid at an auction at a price he knows he can afford.

He swept the book from under his arm and opened it.

'This proves you're a liar, always were and always will be.'

'What are you talking about?'

'All here.' He threw back his head and sniffed.

'You'd believe anything Constance wrote.' I smiled secretly thinking of her comment in her letter. The 'demon' Reynold.

'Constance never lied.'

With what frailty do you say this, dear brother?

'Posterity has to goggle over what Constance wrote years ago then?'

He read:

'"I have decided to marry John Spence. To lead a respectable life. Just as well after Dilly's little misdemeanour."'

'None of us were saints.'

'"Dilly has been allowed to leave the factory because of her condition."'

'I was sacked because I wanted to be sacked. I was under the Control of Engagements Order and you couldn't leave a job unless you were sacked. I deliberately botched my work. I hated the place.'

'All very interesting.'

'So.'

'She says you went to work in a pig farm in Surrey for the last few months.'

I found myself walking round the kitchen, picking up and putting down objects, plates, the kettle I filled from the sink. I poked the range.

An American GI shouts: 'What's cookin', Curly?'

A thick scum of oil works its way up the backs of my black-market stockings. The winter of 1945. And Constance was working away at this villainy.

'I suggest that the last few months means the last few months of your, er, pregnancy.'

'You're crazy. She meant the last few months since her last entry.'

'Do you want to see? It's dated day by day.'

'Well. It could mean anything and I don't care.'

'It'd be quite easy to prove, you know. But I not going to go behind your back and hunt out the records.'

'Why not? Yes, why not?'

Worry your head about something that may or may not have happened in the distant past while a drunken psychopath prowls round the house.

There was no point in staying in the kitchen. I was going out the door when he said loudly, 'Where do you think you're going?'

I shut the door quietly after me.

I stood for a while. The leaves swept the cobbles like old women with brooms. One of the cats whipped through the blade of light.

How long would he sit there gloating? Believing he was being tolerant by his single statement that he would not follow the matter up.

He shouted, 'Dilly'. He can Dilly all he likes. I went further out of earshot.

Then it happened.

An almighty crack and the splintering of glass, a figure darting across the light from the windows, disappearing into the gloom.

I raced into the kitchen. Reynold had the most extraordinary expression on his face.

'Get upstairs, quick,' I yelled.

'What the, what the . . . .' His face was ashen, his mouth a ring, his eyes staring. 'Reynold, quickly, for God's sake. Hurry.'

'I'll go and look.' Reynold was too bemused to stop me.

Everything was quiet now as I raced through McDonagh's fields. Only the tearing of my breath through my chest broke the uncanny silence. When I reached the ruined cottage it was empty. Jesus! I called and called, but there was no answer. I retraced my steps sick with worry.

It was all my fault. If I hadn't encouraged her that first day . . . if I hadn't got involved with her . . . if she hadn't fallen in love with me . . . So I betrayed her, her affection, her need. Horrified,

I went back in.

Reynold was still standing, staring at the broken pane of glass.

Shaking I swept up the splinters, pulled the curtains tight shut.

'What the . . . what the . . .' Reynold kept repeating.

Hot sweet tea for shock. For once I was in control. His terror was so plain to see that I felt almost calm. That was his gesture, one shot, break the window of the lousy Prods. No one can prove it was he.

And, I argued to myself, Cathy can't be in her house, or otherwise he wouldn't have come up here again. Specious, perhaps, but it did much to keep my nerves under control.

I sat Reynold down and gave him a huge cup of hot sweet tea and a shot of whiskey with it.

He drank like a lamb. The blood gradually came back to his face.

I noticed his hand shook badly as he leant over to put the cup and saucer down on the table.

'Thanks.'

Then I heard a scream. And another. It was my name.

I opened the door and there was Cathy. But Cathy in an unrecognisable state. There was blood running down her cheek, a nasty gash over one eye. She was holding her shoulder with one hand and crying in an awful sick animal way.

I brought her in. Naturally I thought he must have shot her. But he hadn't. He had just beaten her. Beaten her badly. Maybe broken her shoulder with something other than his fist.

I picked her up and carried her to the couch.

Reynold started mouthing again and I just told him to shut up and get a cloth and some water.

For a moment he stood looking down at her before doing as I told him.

I bathed her face — the cut needed a couple of stitches. I was afraid to touch the shoulder in case I made it worse.

'Call an ambulance.'

Meekly he went to the passage where the phone is and I heard him calling the local exchange. Thank God for the telephone, was all I could think of.

She opened her eyes and a wave of pain swept across her face. 'Lie quite still,' I whispered. 'You'll be all right.'

Reynold returned, hovered, asked could he do anything. When I shook my head he sat uncertainly, his lips pursed, not quite sure what to do or say next. Clearly my stiff-necked attitude had surprised him and he was afraid to speak.

I mixed pain-killers in water and lifted her to drink. She found it hard to swallow. The time seemed endless. I kept murmuring supportive words, wiping her brow with a warm cloth, straining my ears for the sound of a car. At last it came.

Two men came in carrying a stretcher with a red blanket. With the expertise of their kind they lifted her on and bustled her into the back of the ambulance.

'Where do you think you're going?' He watched me throw on my coat.

'Where do you think? To a disco?'

'Don't be rude!'

The journey to the town seemed extra bumpy, the twelve miles half across the county. But the hospital, when reached, was a small friendly place. The porter, an old man with a dry mouth, directed us up a corridor into a waiting room. There was a worried-looking woman, probably in her late twenties but worn out by the deceiving years. Was she waiting for news of a sick child? She didn't speak, merely smoked, puffing continuously from a king-size cigarette. Her long thin legs, her high-heeled shoes, her short hair and plastic earrings, her combat jacket over the tight jeans, gave her the air of one who still has a spark of hope left which her expression and the constant smoking belied.

We must keep hoping, all of us. I looked at Cathy. Hoping? Why? Her dull hair was matted with mud and sweat, like a wig on the ambulance pillow. Luckily she was asleep — or shocked into unconsciousness. Yes. Hoping!

The registrar was about twenty-eight, smelling of soap, his round pulpy face and baby lips gave the impression of one who is trying very hard to be compassionate in a professional way.

He was gentle with Cathy, murmuring, 'We'll get this stitched.'

And turning to me, 'Are you the mother?' I explained, or tried to.

'Has her mother been informed?'

'Not yet.'

He told me to go into the Sister's office and give all the details. Cathy was wheeled into a ward further down the corridor.

The details?

A drunkard shoots a bullet through my window because he thinks I'm hiding his daughter with evil intent. He then finds the girl and beats her into a pulp, goes home and goes to the pub.

Question: Who am I and how did I get into all this?

Answer: I am an old woman who fooled herself into thinking

she could leave her business, her friends, her lover(s) and come home to spend her last years looking after 70 acres of scrub, water, trees and little hills, using her latent knowledge, energy, adaptability and — most important — her debt to the land while so doing. Lies, all lies, Ms Nurse. She imagined she would make a successful turn, that here the world would acknowledge her worth, the land would roll back for her and receive her with open arms.

Yes, Ms Nurse, that's the he and the she of it.

And the result? I land up in a sea of hostility, befriend a young girl who is the butt of the above gentleman's vainglorious fantasies of being something that matters in the cosmos — in the county — in the country. He carries a gun to make him a person to be reckoned with.

There you have it, Ms Nurse. In a nutshell.

And Mr pulpy-faced Doctor, nice, well-meaning, will do his best — inter alia — to mend a little wound, sew it up nice and tight so the owner of it can live another day.

I suppose in the end I gave some sort of precis of the foregoing because she said, scratching her hair with the biro, 'We live in terrible times.'

I dropped cigarette ash all over the floor and myself as I waited for the guards to come. Neither Reynold nor I had thought of the police, strangely. But a shot is a shot, after all. People in dressing-gowns trod the corridor, a woman ran in carrying a baby. Everyone ran, a trolley rolled, doors closed softly.

Thick in their uniform, they arrived. Two of them.

I went with them down the yellow lit corridor, the linoleum soft under our feet. A uniformed driver sat in the blue car. I was put in the back.

The barracks is a long low building beside the courthouse, a 'listed' 19th century building of which the town is very proud. Business goes on all day and most of the night in or around this place. The colonial pillars and granite portico, prideful of a time past, now reassure citizens that justice still only favours the rich.

The strict discomfort of the long bench on which I was told to sit was made more depressing by the forty-watt bulb and the portentous bearing of the middle-aged guard detailed to take down my statement. With automatic precision he slowly went over my movements during the last four days. With every word his hand described a curve as though he had only lately learned to read and write. Exhaustion crept down and over me till I felt my body had been buried in plaster. Only my mind remained acid clear, my phrases careful, circumspect.

The grilling, the disbelief, the shaded disgust on the guard's face. The mental bullying. Stupid, wasn't it, to bother with such a delinquent.

I wanted to get back to the hospital to check she was all right. They laughed. I ceased to care what they thought. I answered at length, automatically. I knew my lines. I've always known them. I gave them not what they wanted but an assimilation of the facts. They would have liked me to blame Cathy and be high-handed about everything.

The statement down, I was shown the door, thrown literally out into the recondite night.

Extreme exhaustion invents its own rhythm. As the miles unpeeled, the monotony of effort caused my mind to switch into its various channels, plans overlapping each other, and it took quite a while to realise that there was a new night sound, a man-made sound, following me slowly. It was a tractor. A tractor driven by a mere boy.

There was no need to ask him how far he was going, for he had stopped and I found myself astride the cross-bar behind him. Fighting back sleep that would have crept over me like warm water I rode the few miles before he turned into a lane and I once more faced the leaden road ahead. What will he think when day comes, I wondered. That he had actually carried a ghost on his machine? The banshee? In person?

The worst miles, the last, were covered in an ache of muscle and mind. The lad, my saviour, must plough into morning through the drizzle that seems to accompany every occasion these days. My clothes tightened against what then became a downpour, the water rattling and splashing as though determined not to forget the final straw. I did get home, however, by some miracle.

I am writing now in this early morning house, whose walls are as cold as salt. I see the dawn at last creeping up the fields. Another dawn. The rain has stopped. The east glows pink and I am cured by this new day. That is to say I feel very strongly the privilege of being alive.

A bare three hours sleep and up again.

'What time did you get in?'

'Late. Or rather, early.'

'You need your sleep. You shouldn't have gone with that little wretch.'

'Leave it, Reynold.'

'I don't wish to interfere with your affairs. But it is my

responsibility to create an air of respectability in the neighbourhood.'

'Reynold, for God's sake.'

'People round here don't appreciate charitable actions. No doubt you feel sorry for her. She's a pretty pathetic object.'

'I happen to like her. There's nothing charitable about my actions. Should I have left her to die?'

'You know perfectly well what I mean.' Unfortunately I did and if I didn't shut up I'd say the wrong thing. 'You do have the oddest tastes.'

We seldom breakfast together and this was getting more and more awkward.

'I worry about you, Dilly. I often wondered if some treatment would help you along. These places are wonderful nowadays, you know. Not at all primitive. Then once you were fixed up...'

'Fixed up?' I screamed, 'you make me sound like a hoover or something that needs a few parts.'

'No no, Dilly. You'd feel much stronger, much less likely to fall prey to every Tom, Dick or Harry looking for your sympathy.'

How near he skated to the truth but with what evil cunning!

'You want to turn me into a cabbage. You know very well what they do. Fill you up with drugs, change your personality, take away your tensions. What's a person without tensions? A zombie, that's what.'

He shrugged. 'You go your way, then.'

I went out. I had the unfortunate job of going to see Mrs Magee.

'You know who I am?'

'Aye.'

There was Jim and no mistake. The other children had that taking things for granted look on them while Jim was apart. Which is not to say he was retarded or odd in any way. Merely aware — sharp in every sense. He held his head at an angle like one expecting distant sounds, he put his weight on only one leg and while the others fought through the door to get out for school, he followed at a casual pace.

With their absence the kitchen expanded and she sat to face me, the dregs of a cup of tea in her hand.

'She's not bad. She'll be home in a few days, Mrs Magee.'

'She will not.'

We looked at each other. The dark ferocity of the woman was a shock. The black hair cut tight to her head, the arms muscular as a man's with the sleeves rolled to the elbows, the beauty of the firm mouth, small nose, mahogany eyes was unfathomable.

How well she had weathered her appalling life.

'But...?'

'Do you want her killed?'

'That the woman?' The voice came from upstairs. Mrs Magee got up to tidy the debris left by the children. She didn't call up but went to the stove and put on a frying pan, sweeping spilled cornflakes off the table with one hand on to the palm of the other.

He came down the stairs. Before he entered shivers of horror went down my spine and I swivelled round to face him, face the man who so recently could easily have murdered me. He looked awful, spit on his chin which was blue from a quick shave in cold water. He didn't look at me.

'Are ye satisfied now?' he addressed his wife. She shrugged and threw the 'fry' in front of him. He hovered at the table, unable to sit. Twice he tried and twice he was obliged to stand again. The sickness in his stomach showed yellow on his cheeks. He clenched and unclenched his hands. Suddenly he made a dive, sat, and started to eat quickly, each mouthful being washed down with gulps from a mug of tea. When the knock came he banged his chair back from the table.

Their navy-blue uniforms filled the doorway.

'Are you Mr Magee?'

'You've no business interfering in a family row.'

'I'm afraid you'll have to come down to the station for questioning. You Mrs Magee?' She nodded. The younger guard turned on me.

'What's your name?'

'Strong. The men on duty last night took my statement.'

'We'll go so,' the older one said and the three of them left in silence. Once more we sat staring at each other across the table.

'I'm very sorry for all this, Mrs Magee.'

When she didn't reply I said, 'She's ward 6a. The wound isn't serious. It was stitched up last night. She was quite comfortable, they said.'

She got up, climbed a chair by the dresser and reached up to the top shelf. From an envelope she extracted two five-pound notes.

'I doubt I'll have time to go over. Give her these.' With an athletic swoop she jumped to the floor and thrust the money into my hand.

'If there's anything I can ... I'll give ...' my voice ran away in little spurts. Her great cynical eyes absorbed me even as I backed out the door and turned for home.

I had that kind of clear vision one gets from lack of sleep. Going back up the avenue, planes met and divided sharply, angles tidied, the Friesians stared at me with their wide white faces questioning the logic of my passing. A half-hearted day at best, I knew it would rain later. A donkey brayed from far off.

'That's it,' I said out loud.

And of course there was Reynold, forks of frown going and coming between his eyebrows.

He has a habit of bunching the newspaper as he reads it. On my entry he reared up bunching and unbunching as though the paper were a squeeze box.

'Yes?' he said, a world of fume in his tones.

'Yes nothing. I've given the necessary information to the necessary quarter.'

'Have you nothing to say to me?'

I felt like an old motor-car that has been souped up by an enthusiast. Here was Reynold obsessed with delving in the past in order to prove his equation that x in the past equals y in the present while a homicidal maniac tours the grounds. Or will when he gets out on bail.

'About what? Cathy? Mr or Mrs Magee?'

'I don't want to hear anything about your latest sordid associations with undesirables. Just keep your nose clean while you're here, will you?'

'I'll try.'

I felt hopeless.

'I'll go. I'll pack and go tomorrow. Leave you in peace.'

'Take the easy way out, will you?'

'That's the hardest way, Reynold, and you know it.' I left the room.

I thumbed a lift into the town in the bread van.

Cathy was wide awake but there were two noticeable things about her: one, that she wasn't going to die, and two, that she was in great pain.

There was a radio blaring in the ward.

'Walking back to happiness
I threw away
Walking back to happiness
With you ... ooo ... oo ...'

Her eyes were feverish. It would be a few days before she'd be let out.

She looked at the fruit I'd brought her but didn't touch any. She was wound up in bandages and had the apricot tinge of cleanliness you see in hospital wards.

Reynold called her a 'pathetic wretch'. I kissed her forehead. 'You'll be better soon.'

I gave her the two fivers. She looked interested for a moment. 'What'll they do to me da? Will they put him in gaol?'

There was no emotion in her voice. Just curiosity.

'Hard to say. He'll get bail, I'm sure.'

'How's me ma?'

'Strong. Very strong.'

She looked past me as if she didn't care to talk. I sat on a while. Adjusted her pillows to get her more comfortable.

'You're young, you'll heal up quickly.' Useless words.

It was the usual mixture in the ward, very old women mostly. Except for a dark-haired girl in the far corner, about Cathy's age. Her leg was in a cradle, plastered to the toe.

'She fell off her bike,' Cathy said with a twist in her voice as if it were funny.

I left, worried stiff as to how I could help to solve her problem. If the authorities got on the job they might send her to some home or other and that would be the finish of her.

I wandered into town to treat myself to a restaurant lunch. There's an old-fashioned café which seemed preferable to the chipper and I settled for two sausage rolls and coffee. As I sat down I found myself tray to tray with Arthur.

Seeing him was like being met by a search party in the desert.

He didn't waste time. Those Sundays building up to that moment were liked padded steps on a wide staircase. The Central, like all mid-sized town hotels, had the beige and brown silence of corridors and rooms, of shabby polished cheap 1940s dressing tables, whose drawers stick and whose mirrors depress. I don't think either of us looked at each other — I think I drew the curtains, ashamed of my too thin limbs, nor did I want to see any pink of his flesh that was not normally exposed.

But our skins mingled and warmed as we waged our sexual battle beneath the bedclothes, above, below, sideways. Afterwards he looked at me with a sort of humble gratitude when it was I who should have been thanking him. He didn't want to get up. We had vodka and tonics sent up to us, made love again (perhaps less successfully but with a lot of affection and mutterings) and it was after seven and getting dark when we got up and put ourselves in order for the public eye.

'Sorry I wasn't home to make the supper. Something you'll get used to soon.'

'I'll manage.' His head was low. Hard to see his expression.

'I'm sure.'

'How was she?'

'Who?'

'The girl?'

'Fine. Fine.'

'Good.'

'Why are you sitting in the dark?'

'I was thinking. Didn't notice the night falling.'

No no. I'm not going to feel sorry for you now, dear brother. You're going to miss me though, aren't you?

At the corner of the hearth there is a chopper. A fine edged tool, just the right weight for me to manipulate.

If I were to pick it up. If I were ever to pick it up!

I walked towards it. I bent and lifted it slowly, tension gathering in my muscles, stepped slowly towards him then dropped it with a clatter.

'You're no better than Mr Magee,' I shouted.

'Dilly, calm down. You've had a bad time.'

'Really. Oh really. How observant of you.'

Still here. The leaves are turning. Few things left to say. A pleasant Sunday with Arthur. No mention of the day at the hotel. We talked the past over. About Constance. And how now her bones bleach in an unknown grave.

'Did you ever hear what happened to the child?' he said.

I sat up astonished.

'What are you talking about?'

'Surely you knew?'

'Knew what? Arthur, I was away.' My heart had begun to pound, literally. 'What are you saying?'

He seemed mystified at my ignorance.

'The child she had. Before she married Spence?'

'I don't believe it.' I suddenly felt a chill go through me. Could it have been ... no ... I stared at his clear face.

'But who, but who was the father?'

Constance? The Constance whom everybody loved? The Constance who must have burned most horribly to death. My sister Constance. From two separate eggs we emerged. The pretty and the plain.

'McDonagh.'

Scaly, slit-eyed, rough and ready McDonagh, the father of my sister's child? Not he though, it was a blatant youth, with footballer's shoulders, smoky eyes and long arms that'd catch you in the dark. A cracked laugh when you jumped with fright. She took him up to the hayloft to its combustible organic warmth. There they would copulate freely while father believed all the time that his pet, his dove would fly back to his arms.

'Don't leave,' Arthur said.

It is the last few days.

Yes, Arthur did say, 'Don't leave,' but Reynold didn't dare. I knew he wanted to but he just went about his business, head lowered, unable to meet my gaze.

I went to see Cathy for the last time. I told her I was leaving. I couldn't bear the look of anger, hatred almost, that shadowed her features.

She simply turned her head away. I told her that I had arranged everything with her aunt and that her mother was agreeable also. And that I had sent some money on for her keep. Then I handed her an envelope with ten pound notes in it, saying that she would be allowed to leave the following day and that one of the orderlies would escort her to the bus.

Still she didn't speak. She just took the envelope and stuffed it under her pillow.

I left the ward and walked slowly down the corridor.

That's it.

I tell myself that I can start again. Maybe lease a shop in Dublin.

The land! How nearly I made it work.

I leave only a painted room, a mended pane of glass, a dozen hens, a refurbished hen-coop. Dilly's marks!

EPILOGUE

CATHY

Sometimes Cathy thought she might run away. Leave the Centre altogether. For hours she would look out of the window daydreaming, dream that she lived with Dilly, just the two of them on the farm. In her more crazy moments she dreamed of going to the farm and killing Reynold. Then when this action was achieved in her imagination she would sit back contented, watching herself and Dilly feeding the hens, digging the garden, and then when they were exhausted they would have their tea and cake and biscuits, the fire in the old range tearing up the chimney. But her thoughts weren't always as positive as this. There were days when she just stared and thought of nothing. Each day at the Centre another tick on the calendar.

But mostly her nights were filled with demons. She would toss and turn, re-enacting that awful time in the hotel, sometimes shouting out loud Dilly's name.

She hadn't told the doctor everything that had happened that awful night. What she'd done after she'd run from the sittingroom. Nor how she'd shut herself in her room but the man — that dreadful man with Dilly — that Mr Starling — had forced himself in. How at first he'd shoved a magazine under her door with a nude girl shaped like an S in the folded page, crying out 'She's dying for me'. And there he was huge inside her room, unzipped and with his penis holding the tails of his shirt at an angle. How she had screamed at him to go away, to leave her alone, but he only laughed at her. Then when she was wetting the bed she begged to be let go to the toilet and he had said, 'Do it on the bed.'

How had she got away? It was only when Dilly came in. And God how angry Dilly was. Called her a 'fucking little bitch', accused her of 'deliberately turning him on'. And she had told her how much she wanted to be with her and Dilly had cursed her more.

Oh God, she tossed and turned each night, saying over and over, 'If only I'd gone then'. But she hadn't. She still hoped that Dilly would change her mind and leave him, come with her, so she had hidden downstairs until she knew they were in bed and then crept up and into their room.

He was asleep but Dilly was still awake. And she looked so terrible, as though she were in hell, without hope, without any future except this crazy man who didn't care a hoot for her and would probably one day kill her.

'Dilly', she'd whispered, Dilly, but the other had only stared at her, her eyes huge and blank. She had gone over to her, lifted her face and tried to hug, but Dilly just groaned, 'Go away, for God's sake go away, rabbit bones.' And then of course what happened only didn't he wake up and jump out of bed. The next thing Cathy knew was that he was lying over her on the floor and Dilly watching and screaming and she wriggling and trying to get away. And of course he did it, raped her, and then got up and poured a sponge full of water over her, laughing all the time that terrible heavy laughter that seemed to shake the house.

How she had tried to say sorry to Dilly but she couldn't get it out.

This terrible shame and guilt came over her each night as she fought to go to sleep, to forget. Why, oh why, had she gone back? All she ever saw now were Dilly's beseeching eyes, asking her, begging her to leave.

She'd nearly forgotten the rest of the night, waking up in a doorway with a cop looking down at her, telling her to get a move on. She didn't even remember leaving the hotel, all she knew was that she must find the bus station and get out of

Dublin. Somehow or other she must have found it because the next thing she knew her aunt was yelling at her, asking her where the hell she'd been and that she was dead sick of her.

There had been weeks then when she'd gone here and there, in desperation snatched an old one's bag and ended up in the courts, and the bastard of a judge had sent her to the Centre.

And now she was here in this goddamned place, a nothing, a nobody. She just did what she was told. When they told her to go in the garden, she went. When the meals were ready, she sat down and ate them. She didn't talk to the other inmates so they soon forgot about her.

Occasionally the matron would try to interest her in sewing or some board game, but Cathy just stared at her, so she gave up.

One day, as she sat gazing out of the window, she saw a man that reminded her of Reynold. Without thinking she went out and began to follow him. She caught up with him when he stopped to cross the road and she looked right into his face — he was a stranger. Again, without thinking what she was doing, she carried on up the street until she came to the bus depot. There was a bus just about to leave for a town six miles from Mullaghbawn. She boarded it.

Why was she on the bus? What could she say to Mister when she got to the farm? But there was no going back. She knew that she'd never sleep again unless she pleaded with him.

After the long miles of walking once she left the bus, she was more and more abstracted. When she reached the foot of the avenue she didn't recognise it. There was a brand new gate where there had never been a gate before. And the lane wasn't rutted and pot-holed either. It had been tarred and a single electric wire ran up the side of each field. There were more young Friesians in the well field and the hill field was waxy and golden with a crop of barley.

And the yard! The yard was a palace compared with how it used to be. The out-houses were all rebuilt and the hen-house — Dilly's hen-house — had had a run wired on to it and dozens of hens, it seemed, were parading up and down waiting for their feed.

She doubled back to the kitchen and knocked on the door.

Reynold came out at once. But it wasn't like the Reynold she remembered. At first she thought that this man, too, was a stranger, perhaps some German who had bought the place and done it up. But it was him all right. Behind the beard and underneath the Aran sweater and jeans was the same Reynold. The same stiff unyielding Reynold.

He looked at Cathy in amazement.

'Where the hell did you come from?'

'Don't you remember me, Mister?'

'Unfortunately I do. You've not changed much.'

Cathy didn't tell him that she had hardly recognised him but continued nervously. 'It's about Dilly. I come about her, please.' She found it difficult to get the sentences out properly. 'Please, Mister, will you do something about her?'

'Dilly makes her own decisions.'

'Oh Mister, please, you don't know how desperate she is.'

'I suppose she's picked up some undesirable character.' As he said this he walked past her and went off to feed the hens.

Cathy ran after him, not knowing how to convince him. He *must* do something. Send for her. Get her back.

But when she mouthed her plea he merely said: 'My sister's business is none of yours. If she wants to destroy her life I'm not going to interfere. I told her to stay on till spring that time but she wouldn't listen. She goes her way and I'm very happy to go mine. Thank you very much.' And with a sniff he marched back into the house.

Back in the Centre, each blank day followed another. She had given up making plans. Even the nightly horrors had begun to recede. Suddenly she was jolted out of this near-catatonic state. She was told she was to go to see Dr Le Strange again.

'No, I don't want to go.'

They said it was for her own good. She must.

Once again she found herself sitting in the doctor's room on the same old chair, Constance behind her desk.

For the last fortnight Constance had been in a state of intoxication. She only had sporadic moments of lucidity. Her mind was quite fogged up with alcohol.

That crook, Dr McKay, she kept saying to herself, thinks he can bring back my past. He's a fool.

Still she scribbled in her notebook. Her latest entry read: 'I used to be great fun.' Now why did I write that, I wonder? Fun. I used to have great fun.

She looked now across the room at Cathy. She has something to do with this, she thought. To do with her? With this fun business . . .

Cathy had been sent to her. She needed Cathy.

She got up and paced. No no, she kept repeating.

Suddenly she said: 'Cathy, you never finished your story.'

The latter burst into tears, her shoulders heaved, 'Oh God, Miss,' she muttered, 'She called me Rabbit bones.'

'Who did?'

'Dilly. When I went to her room.'

'Dilly,' Constance shouted. 'I'm sick and tired of this Dilly. Can you think of nothing else?'

'But she loved me, I know she did. Why oh why did she send me away?' She'd stopped crying and was looking at Constance vacantly.

'What do you want me to do?'

'Find her. Please. She'd listen to you.'

'No, she wouldn't.'

'How do you know?'

'Draw people away from their obsessions? What a hope.' Constance took a swig and sat down again.

'She'll be killed, miss.'

'Probably.'

'You are cruel. You don't care about anything.'

'No. Not cruel. I just came to a full stop one day. And you, you have no disease, you fall into no category. But you, too, have come to a stop. Like an old car. You could push it up and down hill forever but if the engine's fucked it'll never start. You are a decent void, Cathy, but you have been sent here to cure me. Welcome.' Constance was making a great effort now to see straight. 'She left you, this Dilly, discarded you like an old coat. You may think I'm bad. Ah but, I've a store of knowledge hidden in some cubbyhole of my brain. And it's your job, Cathy, to drag it out.'

She got up and went over to the young woman. She took her two shoulders and began to knead them. 'Mm . . . Rabbit bones. It suits you. This old woman who loved you . . . was . . . was' Suddenly she screamed. 'Dilly. There are two girls, one of them is me and the other is you, Cathy . . . we are playing . . . Oh God. Fun. Great fun . . .' she ran back to her seat and put her hands up to her face. 'Oh God, Oh God,' she was muttering . . . 'I don't know . . . She lusted . . . lusted for the land. Who did? Cathy! You must help me.' Her voice was high and she was thumping her desk with her fist.

Cathy was terrified. She suddenly realised the awful agony Constance was going through was quite different from her normal cynical condition. She wanted to help her but had no strength or knowledge left. She stayed staring in front of her.

'You'd better go now,' Constance muttered. 'It's no use.'

This wasn't the last time Cathy saw the doctor. Once more she was sent for. But this time Constance was really tucked away in some crazy other world.

'Ah ha,' she said when Cathy entered. 'I was just admiring my legs and thinking they were of no importance nowadays. Marlene Dietrich walked legs first into Hollywood. And you are?'

'Cathy.'

'Oh yes,' Constance laughed coarsely. 'My cure.'

Cathy began to tell her about her visit to the farm, her conversation with Reynold. How she had begged him to get Dilly home where she belonged.

But Constance didn't seem to be listening although she said vaguely,

'Oh, Reynold, he wasn't very nice, was he?'

'I wish you'd listen,' Cathy was desperate.

'Oh yes. But I wanted to tell you something. Yes. About Sappho. Have you ever heard of Sappho?'

'No.'

'She lived long long ago. She was a poet. Eros the Dawn has arms like roses, brings light to the ends of the earth. Yes, she lived in an island called Lesbos.'

'You think I'm one of those?'

'Really? Do you not want to be loved? Stroked? Held? Your body exhausts itself for this need. That's why old people die.'

Constance left her chair and came round to where Cathy sat. She pulled her up and took her in her arms. She stroked her hair and kissed her neck. 'You did well,' she murmured, 'Think well of yourself. You tried. One day you will run in the woods again. A dryad from the bole of a tree.'

She lifted her up and placed her on the desk. Slowly she removed Cathy's stockings, her knickers, and placed one finger in her vagina. She drew the cushion of her forefinger up towards the palpitating clitoris.

The orgasm flooded through Cathy. Wave upon wave. She moaned and tossed with it, stretching her arms towards Constance, pulling her down for an extended kiss.

Constance dragged herself away and Cathy fell back only to jump up immediately, snatching her clothes and frantically putting them on.

She ran to the other side of the room, not knowing where to look. She knew that Constance was angry, could see it in her back.

She didn't know what to say. Suddenly she blurted out: 'Dilly thought you was dead.'

'Oh that,' was all Constance muttered.

Cathy wanted the other not to be angry. Like Dilly she wanted her back to her old self. For surely Constance had an old self somewhere. She watched her filling up her glass and gulping down the brandy. She was murmuring too, 'She hates calling me Constance. A constant person is one who is faithful in love and friendship.'

Cathy jumped on this. 'Oh yes. She was constant to Reynold. Always. And,' she continued:

'And he has hens now. How Dilly would love to see the place again.'

'Would she?'

'Oh, you don't understand. You have never understood how Dilly cared. She cared for me too.'

Constance looked closely at her. She suddenly knew. She said very slowly: 'Dilly lusted . . . she lusted for the land and when she couldn't have that she . . .'

'What, oh what, tell me . . .'

'Tell you,' the doctor's head had dropped. 'I've nothing to tell you . . . I don't know who you're talking to . . . about . . . I mean.'

'And he loved the hens . . . I could see . . . He talked to them . . . cluck cluck cluck . . .'

Constance said without looking up: 'A little ceremony each day. Like what you've just experienced. A little death . . . How charming . . . Jean Genet . . . What did you say?'

'Nothing.'

'I remember . . . oh yes, I remember . . . in his onanistic writings he called the orgasm a little death . . . Did you know that?'

'No, miss.'

'I was married once. To a man called Justin. Well, I was married twice actually but the first time didn't count. He's dead. And ever since then? A fucking calendar of celibacy. That's what.'

Cathy tried very hard to follow what the other said but the accustomed lethargy was creeping over her. It was as though she were shredded in half — formless. She longed to feel different, to feel strong.

Constance had her head in her hands again.

Cathy levered herself up and crept toward the door. On the threshold she was called. The doctor was holding out a piece of paper she had torn from her notebook.

She took it and left.

Cathy continued to live at the Centre, gradually becoming more and more institutionalised. She will probably live there forever.

When she got back that day, before tearing it up, she read the note. It said: 'I can only say *there* we have been: But I cannot say how long, for that would be to place it in time.'